My Thanks to Pearl Popper Shapira
for her help with my book.

MURDER
ON
STAGE

WRITTEN BY
ZIPORA PELED

iUniverse, Inc.
New York Bloomington

Murder On Stage

iUniverse books may be ordered through booksellers or by contacting:

iUniverse
1663 Liberty Drive
Bloomington, IN 47403
www.iuniverse.com
1-800-Authors (1-800-288-4677)

ISBN: 978-1-4502-2813-8 (pbk)
ISBN: 978-1-4502-2814-5 (ebk)

Printed in the United States of America
iUniverse rev. date:3/24/11

CHAPTER ONE

I knew my body was up. I was hoping my mind would catch up but it's not going to cooperate.

It's only plugged into about 10% of its power and that grudgingly.

Just enough so I won't bump into my furniture when I get out of bed.

Who wants to get out of bed?

Oh, the hell with it. I've functioned mindlessly before, I can do it again.

I pulled back the covers and sat on the edge of the bed.

Glancing at the clock, I am stunned. It's not even 7:00 o'clock!

I'm an actress, in Habima, the Israeli National Hebrew Theater in Tel Aviv, the most impressive theater in Israel. I'm not supposed to get up this early and try to cope with life, for Pete's sake!

That's one of the perks of working for the theater.

Then I remembered...the murder...it must be the murder. I was whacked out last night and, contrary to my usual habit, I went to sleep before midnight.

I was standing right beside her on the stage when it happened. She was my stage manager.

We were discussing the scenery for the new show when that large weight came hurtling down from above.

Everyone was stunned and for a moment nobody moved,,,then pandemonium.

Everyone asked if I was alright.

I remember someone screaming...was that me?

This was someone I knew who was lying there with her head smashed in and blood pouring out.

==========

The only dead body I had seen in all my life was a boy who was a student in my high school class in Cass Technical High School in Detroit, Michigan in the USA.

He was killed in an accident. That was a shock also.

I saw him get out of the taxi after the accident and he was laughing.

The next morning they announced that he had died from internal injuries.

I can still see that young man lying in the coffin.

==========

Someone shouted: "Call an ambulance."

Someone else shouted: "It's too late, call the police!"

Someone brought me a chair and told me to sit in it.

Someone else brought me a glass of water. That was thoughtful.

That must have been me screaming.

Someone put a jacket around me.

I was shaky and trembling. I sat in that chair frozen...my mind refusing to accept what had happened, until the police arrived.

When the police came, they questioned everyone and especially me.

Ben Arden was a detective from the homicide squad. He was nice. Not too tall or too fat, with blond, curly hair, a ruddy complexion, a small nose, an ordinary likeable face.

I even liked his wrinkles. Maybe especially them. They made me feel superior because I didn't have any yet. Men can have wrinkles and look good, darn it.

His brown suit looked worn but it fit him and his tan shirt was crisp and clean and his green socks and green tie made his whole attire look smart.

I really must have been in shock if this is the way my mind was working.

Ben was the detective in charge and he was sure that I was meant to be the victim.

What a horrible thought. It can't be true. Who hated me enough to want to kill me? Ben said that everyone thought that way.

It's true that we moved before the bar fell on Ruth and that might have brought it down on her instead of me.

Ben asked me to go home and write my life story.

"Why do I have to write my life story?" I asked him.

"So that I can find out who had it in for you. I have too much on my plate to waste my time in sitting and questioning you."

"I can tell you right now...nobody!"

"Sure, and this is just a madman who was doing it for fun?"

"Yeah, what else could it be?"

"No, it doesn't look like it. It has all the earmarks of a cleverly planned operation. So you go home and sit down and write your whole life story. The whole nine yards. Especially all your relationships with people," he commanded.

"Alright! But you don't know what you're asking for. My life had not been one smooth road."

"You can record it if you don't want to write it."

"No, I prefer writing it. I'll get all mixed up if I dictate it. Writing it on my computer, I can change the words if I'm confused."

So now I'm stuck with what's going to be a long, long tale of woe. The funny part is that I don't believe that I was the intended victim. Or maybe I don't want to think I'm the intended victim because that's not funny at all.

No, I really think that they wanted to kill Ruth and I'm going to look into it. But first I have to write my life story and believe me, it's like a soap opera the things that happened to me!

I only hope that when I finish with all this, I don't find out that Ben was right.

They canceled the performance when the bar fell on Ruth. I was shaky but I could have gone on.

What ever happened to the saying 'The show must go on"?

Not in Habima, the theater where I was working. They liked any excuse to lay off.

After all, the government pays the deficit so why should the theater worry?

Last year the deficit was 11 million shekels (about 3 million dollars).

CHAPTER TWO

Okay, Fran, drag those bones out of bed and get to work. I tried hard not to think of what I had seen last night.

Poor Ruth with her head crushed in lying on the floor beside me.

Her long black hair had fallen over her face, thank goodness, so I didn't have that to look at.

Some of her brains had splashed on me and some of it had been oozing out on the floor and under my shoes.

I would have liked to throw all the bloody clothes and shoes away but I didn't have that kind of money. So I dragged myself home all bloody.

It was evening so nobody saw me as I dashed home.

I lived five minutes away from the theater so I didn't take a taxi.

When I reached home I took off my new blue trouser suit and soaked it in cold water. That's supposed to coagulate the blood so that it washes off. Then I washed it but the blood stains didn't all come out.

I don't think I'll ever wear that suit again even though it was the first time I had ever worn it.

After that I wiped and shined my shoes.

As I worked I remembered Ruth. I could still picture her lying there. That vision would probably haunt my dreams.

She didn't usually wear any make-up although she wasn't much older than I was. A little make-up would have enhanced her regular features.

Lying there on her back, I saw something that I had never noticed before. Ruth had a lovely figure. The loose knit black garment that she wore had concealed it. Now the material clung to her body and revealed it.

I wondered why she had never tried to make herself attractive.

CHAPTER THREE

Coffee! Coffee! Don't think about it until you've at least drunk some coffee or you'll lose everything that you ate all yesterday. Which isn't so bad when you're on a diet (as always) but the sick nauseous feeling. Ichs! Who needs it?

I made myself the one good cup of real Turkish coffee, filtered that I drink every morning and I went out on the roof to drink it.

The aroma was delightful, especially with the Hel in it. No. that's not a misspelled swear word. It's the Arabic name for the herb – Cardamon. The rest of the time I drink decaffeinated coffee made without chemicals by the Swiss Water method.

I'm a good girl, I am.

I'm living in my new little one room studio apartment around the corner from the Habima Theater where I'm currently engaged as an actress. When our family's tile factory was in danger of bankruptcy, I sold my beautiful three bedroom apartment in Haifa that overlooked the Mediterranean Sea to try and save the factory. It didn't save the factory but at least we paid all the workers and all of our debts and didn't go into bankruptcy and I didn't have that on my conscience. I can just imagine going through the rest of my life with the family's collective finger pointing at me and blaming me for the business failing.

When we paid all the workers off, I only had enough money left to buy this place. I had just moved into it a few days ago.

==========

The apartment in Haifa had a picture window overlooking the lovely Mediterranean Sea below...the first such window in Israel where all the other apartments had a porch in front.

I also had made all the closets built in and with concrete walls and with a window so that I didn't have to take the clothes out and air them. This was a solution to the damp sea air that mildewed the wooden closets.

Many others copied my ideas after that.

I was so sorry to lose that lovely apartment. I had designed it and the theater had given me a few thousand shekel bonus to build it because living in Haifa was considered something of a sacrifice for an actor as the theater center for Stage and Screen was in Tel Aviv.

CHAPTER FOUR

But here I was with my tiny one room apartment and with all the furniture, my lovely sofa and chair, my orange rug, my curtains and pillows wet and dripping. I had left them out on the roof last night and my stinking luck, it rained. The roof, on the 4th floor came with the apartment and I had thought I would have a lovely place to sit when I fixed it up.

That's the down side. But the rain has made the air so fresh that breathing was a joy and every leaf glistened.

There's a beautiful prayer in my prayer book that says it much better that I ever could.

"Oh Lord, let the reviving rains send forth their fragrance to make fertile the earth, to nurture the green herbs, to foster the pleasant fruits and to strengthen the buds. Send rain upon the tender shoots, and let cool waters flow. Sustain the world which Thou hast founded, yea, save our earth, suspended in space."

I like those prayers. I hate the ones which say: "Thou callest the dead to immortal life." It seems to promise what it cannot deliver. Of course some people explain that by saying it means spiritual life... maybe.

Yes, I go to the synagogue on some Saturday mornings. It's a conservative one and I like the sermons that the Rabbi gives us. They're in English and he usually talks about the current topics in a way that binds them with our religion. Not that I agree with him on everything but his sermons don't put me to sleep.

After wards, we pray and sing and then we meet in the patio for wine and cake and social chats. If it's a Bar Mitzva -(The celebration when a boy reaches the age of 13 and becomes a man) we have a regular lunch with herring which I love.

Then a bunch of us go to the King's Hotel across the way and have lunch or just coffee and discuss everything that's happened lately. The lunch that we have is a joke. Two people share an inexpensive dish that has two mounds of Tuna Fish Salad and some vegetables. The brown bread is plentiful and served with real butter. We had our dessert first at the synagogue.

It's supposed to be healthier to have your sweet first. That's because otherwise the sugar sits on top of your food and ferments. Can't you just picture it? Ichs!

If I looked hard enough, I could just see a corner of the theater building from the roof of my apartment. But then I turn around and look at the mess the rain has made of my rug and my furniture.

Why had I ever done such a foolish thing? Probably because the rug had to be cut down and I wanted to give the place a good cleaning before I arranged everything inside.

Now I'm going to have to take it all in and live with the smell of wet wool until I'm sure the rainy season is over and I can put everything out in the sun. I suspect that will be a good few months.

CHAPTER FIVE

This apartment is built in the Bauhaus style as most of Israel is. It's a straight style with everything rectangular. The windows, the doors, even the building itself.

Thank goodness they have finally seen the light and are building with a few arched windows and curved walls. One of the nice features of the law on apartments and home buildings is that it's considered a criminal act to cut down a tree without government permission. Most of the buildings, like mine, are built on stilts with a lawn and flowers underneath and a few trees around the house.

What I would really like to do is throw all the furnishings out! It's a good thing I can restrain myself and not throw things away or I'd never have enough to live on.

The sight was depressing so I went inside to my empty room which held my bed, my TV, my computer and printer and my chair and finished my breakfast.

Wheat toast with white goat's cheese and Zater on top of it. Zater is an herb called Hyssop in English and it's supposed to be the herb that Jesus used for inner cleansing. It does clean out your liver and prevents or fades those brown spots that older people get.

By now you probably noticed that I like herbs. I do! I'm a kind of a health nut. I love to study nutrition and use fresh vegetables, lots of fish, vitamin supplements, herbs, exercise, Thai Chi and Transcendental Meditation to improve my health. Why not? I think it's better than waiting around a doctor's office and suffering illnesses.

Enough fooling around. I guess I just don't want to write about my life. I'll try to convince Ben that he wouldn't learn anything from opening that can of worms.

The trouble is I'm convinced they didn't want to murder me.

I think that Ruth was really the target.

Why do I think this? Just a gut feeling that I have. I can't explain it.

CHAPTER SIX

Zippori MY REPRESENTING ISRAEL

My name is Frances Gillian. I am 48 years old, (I don't feel it and I'm told I don't look it.) Most people think I'm about 30 something and so I can play younger parts on the stage.

I'm a little plump but with a good figure (I'm told that 'zavtik' is the word they use to describe me). I have blue eyes and blond hair. Alright, so I touch it up but it really was naturally blond. The trouble is that I had lighter blond streaks on top when that wasn't the fashion so I started dying it to make the color even and I had to keep it up.

My small nose is definitely not a Jewish nose but my blue, sad eyes do look Jewish. My eyes pop a little and I have a longish chin.

My complexion is good though and I always have color in my cheeks.

I don't exactly know if I could call myself attractive although I am photogenic. I'm told I look a lot like Jane Fonda.

So does my daughter. She had Jane Fonda's tall slender figure too. Her father, my first husband, was six feet tall.

==========

I don't exactly know where in Poland) I was born. For some reason my Mother never wanted to tell us much about our life in Poland. I learned a little from my father but he, too, was reticent about any details.

MYSELF AT 4 YEAR'S OLD IN POLAND

Myself holding a Dog in Poland

MY MOTHER HOLDING ME IN
POLAND

MY FATHER IN POLAND

MY MOTHER AND FATHER

MY UNCLES AND AUNTS

MY RELATIVES – SEATED MY UNCLE
THE SQUEALER

My first memory was living in Warsaw, Poland, in the section that they later called the Warsaw Ghetto – 22 Mila Street to be exact, which is in the same group of buildings as '18 Mila'. That's the name of Leon Uris's book about the Warsaw Ghetto. I remember a kind of circular courtyard opening that I looked down on from our third floor apartment. At first I remembered it as a hollowed out circular building but after I went to Poland, a few years ago, I saw that there were some buildings built in a circle around a yard. That reminds me of where I lived.

All that was left of the Warsaw Ghetto was a piece of wall stuck on another wall commemorating it. I have never met anyone who had lived in the Warsaw Ghetto. I had heard that they were all slaughtered.

I understand that we were quite wealthy before I was born.

Wouldn't you know it! I have photos of all of us all dressed up and a really beautiful and expensive portrait of me when I was four years old.

Our apartment was one large room, a kitchen with two sinks where we washed ourselves, our clothes and the dishes and a toilet that was just a wooden addition that you could hardly squeeze into. Grandmother, grandfather, mother, brother and I lived in the large room. Three of the beds arranged around the wall were double two story bunks so that we all fit in.

My father was in the army. When he came to visit us and anyone would enter the apartment, he had to hide in back of the fur closet because he was home illegally.

Mother had a lot of beautiful furs from when they were wealthy.

Men had to serve 15 years in the army. I have pictures of my father with his hair marcelled. My younger son looks just like him.

If I looked in the mirror of the vanity that stood between the only two windows in the apartment, my grandfather, to discourage me, would say that something might jump out and attack me if I looked in the mirror too long.

And if I went to the bathroom in the middle of a meal, my grandfather would hide my dish and say that my brother had taken it.

He was a jolly man, very religious and with a long white beard. He made rum filled chocolate figures for a living in that one room and I got to lick the bowl!

He used to have a wood shop but no one ever told me what became of that. I remember that once my mother told me that when she was very young and watching the wood shop, a man came in to buy some wood and told her to make out the receipt for four times the amount he bought even though he only paid for one part. She went to her mother and asked what she should do. Her mother told her to do what the man said and after wards explained that everybody did it..

That's why when the Czar wanted to equip his men for fighting the revolution, he didn't have enough supplies.

This is one of the few stories she ever told me about her life.

I remember throwing stones at a boy who came with his pigs in the woods on our property.

I remember looking down out of the window of our third floor apartment when a man with a monkey and an organ came to entertain us. We didn't have an extra penny to throw down to him and that made me very sad.

I also remember reciting and dancing to a song about a butterfly. I guess I always wanted to be an actress.

CHAPTER SEVEN

I had many uncles and aunts. Some came to America and some came to England and one even came here to Israel. He lived in Menara, a kibbutz (that's a commune) on the top western border with Lebanon.

He died of pneumonia while helping the illegal immigrants swim to shore during the Holocaust when the British wouldn't allow the Jewish people escaping from Hitler to come in to Israel legally.

I heard that my Grandfather died before the Holocaust, thank goodness. The rest of my relatives and my grandmother were all killed by the Germans. Maybe that's why I can't see a movie or read a book about the Holocaust or even go into a museum dedicated to that subject.

While in the University, I saw a real movie made in a concentration camp. The man was carrying a woman who was half naked, dressed only in a blouse and so thin she looked like a piece cardboard over his shoulder. I still have nightmares about that movie.

==========

Oh, sitting here on this hard chair and writing all this awful stuff isn't easy. I think I'll stop and clean up the place a little.

Hey, writing is a good way to get things done. You get so fed up with the writing that you want to stop it and move around.

So I went and washed my bloody clothes again. Not that it helped. The bloody stains still wouldn't come out. I don't think I would wear that blue suit again anyway. I don't think I could bear wearing it. It would only make me remember Ruth lying there.

But I better get back to my story. Now where was I? Oh, yes, in Poland.

===========

Well, we left that country when I was six and joined my father in Canada. He had left when I was born. It was easier to immigrate to Canada than the USA.

My mother told me that she had sold all her jewelry and told my father to leave for America.

He deserted the army and succeeded in arriving in Canada. My mother, brother and I came over six years later in steerage on a boat.

I remember eating watermelon for the first time. I also remember a terrible storm.

When we arrived, my father first took us to live in Windsor, Ontario in Canada. Then he took us, illegally, to live in Detroit, Michigan which is right across the border.

Anybody could come from Canada to the USA for a visit but you weren't supposed to stay there.

Staying in Michigan was what made all kinds of trouble for us later.

I started school in Ontario and transferred to grammar school in Detroit, Michigan.

My brother who was one and a half years older than me was two grades ahead of me.

After wards, I skipped a grade. I guess I was kind of clever.

My marks were very good even though I played hooky and often went to the matinees in the theater. Or I went shopping. I still remember seeing Frederic March and his wife Florence Eldridge in 'Long Days Journey into Night'.

When I sent home my purchases C.O.D. (Cash on Delivery) my mother was so curious to see what I had bought that she accepted the packages and paid for them.

I remember she bought me a fur coat once and then mostly wore it herself. She was always doing that...wearing my coats and accessories.

I was absent from school so many days that they wanted to expel me but they couldn't because my grades were so good.

I was chosen to appear in many radio programs and plays that the school put on. That was thanks to my father. When we first saw him at the railroad station in Canada, I was only six and I wanted to talk to him but he said that he wouldn't talk to me until I knew English and we never talked in Polish. He did that so we wouldn't have a foreign accent and he was right. The sad part is that I have forgotten Polish completely. I don't even know one word in Polish.

Many years later I made a movie with Sophia Loren, as her friend and I played the part with a Polish accent.

It started as a joke. I came to the set and I heard the director, Daniel Mann, say that he needed an actress with a Polish accent.

I was very good at accents so I went to him and said in an accent:

"Mr. Mann, I was born in Poland and I speak very good English but I do have a little accent.

He hired me and my contract was $25,000 plus $500 a week for expenses!!!

Sophia, was a lovely person and I hated fooling her. We sat and talked all the free time on the movie. She even gave me her recipe for spaghetti and told me all about her life.

THIS PICTURE WAS NOT FROM THE MOVIE. SOPHIA DANCED JUST TO ENTERTAIN US.

SOPJA LOREN AND ME   THE MOVIE

' JUDITH'

I had a stand in and a make up man and felt very important especially when the director praised my work and wrote in more scenes for me.

Sounds good, huh? I should have gone on to a wonderful career? Uh, huh, not with my luck.

Carlos Ponti, Sophia's husband, came to the set and saw the movie and took out my scenes as much as he could. Why? Who knows?

I like to think it was because I was so good in that part. After all, the director, Daniel Mann, had praised me.

Anyway, Sophia won't release the movie for the distributors.

She's very good in some movies but this wasn't a good part for her.

Sam, an actor who always made trouble for me, told Sophia that I was faking the accent a day before we finished the movie and I was going to tell her myself. She wouldn't talk to me after that.

And to make the whole nine yards bad, just then Israel devalueated the currency and I had to put all the money I earned into paying the whole price of the apartment or else I would have lost it and a lot of money.

Which I lost anyway when I had to sell the apartment in order to save the factory.

CHAPTER EIGHT

"Hi Frances," Ben greeted me cheerfully when I met him at the entrance to the theater. I guess he had been waiting for me. What did he have to be so cheerful about?

Today his suit was a dull blue and pressed. He really looked elegant.

"I hope you did what I asked you to do," he said.

I gave him what I had written and he looked it over.

"Look, Ben," I tried to explain my meager notes. "It isn't easy to write my life story. So much has happened to me and so much of it was unpleasant that it's hard for me to write about it. With my ability to visualize anything I'm reading or writing, it's difficult to do this.

You mean that a lot of people could have wanted to kill you?" he asked eagerly.

"No, I can't even find one who might have wanted to do that. Maybe you'll have better luck.

That's alright. I hope you'll be able to show me something before the week is up." he comforted me. "What you've got here doesn't look too bad."

"I haven't even reached the time that I came here to Israel."

"Do you think it might go better if I asked you questions?"

"No, I but I don't have any rehearsals or any shows this week so I'll have all day to write. The only trouble is, I have a new computer," I added. "That's one of the people I would like to kill,"

"We don't need that!"

"I mean the teacher that I had who took money from me for doing nothing but mess up my programs. He made me so frustrated until finally, with the help of friends, I straightened it all out."

"Now I'm fine but I still boil when I think of that robber. Maybe I'll put a curse on him like I did to someone else who messed with me and the curse worked."

"I'd particularly like to hear about that. That might be the clue I'm looking for.

"No, he's been out of the country making a movie. He couldn't have done it himself and I don't think he's the type that would open himself up to blackmail by letting someone else do it. And he doesn't even know I put a curse on him."

"You never know. He might have something so damaging on that person that he could make him do the murder."

"I'll include him in my notes. Do you have any idea who did it?"

"No, I'm trying to find out who, exactly, could have been up there to make that bar fall."

"I thought you got that information yesterday!"

"No, some of the workers had left for the day so we kept the murder out of the news and I investigated it this morning."

I suppose you found out that it couldn't have been an accident?"

"That's the first thing I looked for. It was impossible. The man who usually ties those bars into place had left before the murder but he showed me that it couldn't have been an accident. The ropes had been cut!"

"That's too bad! That would have been just luck that I wasn't under it at the time but if it was intentional, so......"

"....so, it still was luck that you weren't under it, don't you think?"

I must have looked skeptical.

"You still don't think it was meant for you? Most people think that nobody hates them enough to kill them. But sometimes, it's not hate, you're just in somebody's way or you know something that you might reveal accidentally and ruin that person's life. So keep on writing your story and I'll try to find it, okay?"

"Alright," I told him half - heartedly.

"How about my coming up to your apartment and reading what you're writing while you write it? My being there might keep you writing. What do your say?"

"No thank you, you would just distract me."

I suspected that it wasn't just my writing he was after.

I liked him but I just wasn't ready to be involved in an affair with Ben. My husband and I had separated but I didn't know Ben well enough yet to commit myself.

He really was nice and I was attracted but I wanted to see him a few more times.

Also I didn't want him to prevent me from talking to Ruth's parents and friends and to try and figure out just what had happened and if it really was meant for me.

"Okay, Fran, I'll see you at the funeral. How about going out to dinner with me after wards? That will save you time preparing the meal, right?"

"Not really, I always prepare a few days in advance."

Ben was stymied and all he could say was:

"Okay, so we'll meet here day after tomorrow at the same time?"

"Give me a few days so I can write more that just a few pages. I have other things to do."

"Like what?"

"Not that's it any of your business but I have a check-up at a doctor's and I have to have my hair done and take care of my clothes and my apartment, see my lawyer and so on. Don't worry, I'll work on it every free hour.

"Okay!" he said, trying to sound content with what I said. "I'm glad to see you're finally taking this seriously

I was but not in the direction that he meant.

I liked that he never pressed me too hard. He just put out feelers and, when I didn't take him up on them, he just let it go.

I guess he didn't lack for women who would be glad to have him pursue them. I also wanted more time to find out who Ruth's friends were and visit them. Maybe one of them could tell me if Ruth was afraid of anything.

I just hoped that Ben or some of the other policemen didn't catch on to what I was doing and try to stop me.

"Here's my telephone numbers," Ben handed me his card. "Don't leave it too long. By the way, be careful, this guy might try again."

I looked at him and smiled.

"Okay, so you don't believe me...but be careful. So let's meet on Sunday, (Sunday is just a regular day in Israel - the first day of the week.) You'll have the weekend to work in. Or are you religious?"

"Not at all! But don't start me on that or I won't stop. I'll just tell you that when I think of all that has been done in the name of this or that religion and is still being done, I hate the whole idea of organized religion and I think that prayers should be private, preferably said under a tree or in your own house and the rules should be left up to each individual.

I feel that we are born with God inside ourselves and what we do with our Godliness is up to us.

Tom Paine, the American rebel who fought against tyranny and injustice, in 'The Age of Reason' said it just right:

'I do not believe in the creed professed by the Jewish church, by the Roman church, by the Greek church, by the Turkish church, by the Protestant church, or by any church that I know of. My mind is my own church!'.

Some of the worse slaughter and trouble in the world - now and in the past - has been done in the name of organized religion.

"Here, in Israel we experience it at first hand by the fundamentalist Muslims. Their Koran says that it's okay to kill infidels (anyone who isn't a Muslim) So what kind of religion is that? Most of the terrorists are Muslims. They don't mind dying because they have been brainwashed to believe that if they kill an infidel, they'll go to heaven and be surrounded by beautiful virgins. The family is given money and they celebrate his action and death with a big party when they learn what he has done. And that's all I'm going to say for now, but after this is all over, I'll be glad to discuss it with you again."

"I'd like that. I feel the same way so we should get together. I think we have a lot in common," he said with a seductive smile.

Oh,oh, take it easy. He's really hitting on me.

"I'll bet you say that to all the women you meet, Ben." I say. "See you tomorrow at the funeral."

I didn't give him time to answer that stupid cliche and dashed off to the office to find Ruth's address.

When I go to her house for the funeral, I'm going to try to ask Mrs. Schwartz, her mother, who her friends were and how to get in touch with them. It's going to be touchy with Ben there and some more police but I'll find a way.

I'll tell her and the others that I'm just trying to help the police find the murderer. That's the truth, as far as it goes. I hope they'll talk to me. After all who am I and what authority do I have? Well, I'm an actress. I'll just put on a good act.

I should go to the theater and talk to the stagehands, too. They should know something. They're always the first to know what's up.

Anyway, I've got to eat, and rest.

I reached home, took a fast shower, fixed a salad and a sandwich and got into something comfortable.

To calm myself, I turned on the TV.

If there's any retribution at all in this world, or any justice, TV executives should spend all of eternity watching their own reruns.

Before I went to sleep, I dashed off a few pages so I wouldn'tfeel so guilty.

CHAPTER NINE

My brother, Ralph was a very good actor and appeared in many of the school plays and radio programs.

He was even chosen to play one of the leading roles in a movie with Mitzie Green.

I also remember him in the play, 'Journey's End', where a whole ton of earth came down in front of the actors and was made to look as if it had covered them. Cass Technical High School was a very modern school and had the equipment to put on plays like that.

I was also chosen to act in a few plays but I wasn't as good as my brother.

He was only a year and a half older and was handsome and superior in everything.

While I worked hard to learn to play a musical instrument, he could pick up almost any one of them and play them by ear.

That used to discourage me from going on with my violin or piano lessons.

His grades were excellent and my mother adored him.

My father was my friend. Sometimes we would take the day off, just my father and me and go to a movie. One time we went to a movie and when we came out my father said:

"That wasn't so hot, let's go to another one!" And that's what we did!

We found another movie house and we had some ice-cream until the program started and we went right in.

That was seven hours of programs because each program was a double feature plus a stage show plus a chapter of a continuous adventure series that they showed in those days.

When I was nine, my father got me a job acting in the play, 'The Trial of Tom Mooney',

He knew how much I wanted to be an actress.

Even in Poland I remember all of my early photos show me posing like a model, even at the age of four.

My father was an electrical contractor and was doing a job in that theater when he heard they needed a young violin student for the opening scene.

I was only on stage for five minutes but it was exciting.

Somehow, because I appeared early in the evening, my father and I managed to keep it a secret for two weeks. Then my mother found out about it and that was the end of that. In her opinion, an actress was no better than a prostitute. She was born in the end of the last century and that was the way people thought then.

She still thought like that when we came here to Israel but it didn't help her. By now I was too determined and too strong. She never told people that I was an actress. Once, when we met Ben Gurion, who was the Prime Minister at that time, my mother introduced me as a schoolteacher, as I was the first few years in Israel.

The stork fouled up badly when he dropped me on my folks – neither of whom could do a soft shoe worth a lick. I should have been born in a trunk backstage.

Darn lazy bird couldn't look around a little for two Jewish actors. It flew right past the theater and found two people with a very low priority for acting.`

CHAPTER TEN

I didn't really want to go to the funeral. I hated funerals, especially Jewish funerals where the body is not put in a casket but is carried on a stretcher covered by a white sheet and you could see the outlines of the wrapped body underneath it. It is slid into the grave and covered with earth.

Of course it rained that day. Most of the funerals I have been at have been rained on.

It's fitting. We weep and the sky weeps with us.

When we got to the cemetery, for Ruth's funeral, they wouldn't let the women come to the edge of the grave. Some silly religious law. To me, those rules are what the men made up just to make them feel more important than the women.

If you examine the rules of the fundamentalists of Islam or of our own Jewish orthodox, you'll see very clearly that they put the woman in an inferior position which suits the men because most of them haven't the strength or the power to do it themselves.

We came back to the house and I murmured suitable words to Ruth's parents.

I really meant them but so many people say them at a time like this that they begin to lose all meaning.

I had some coffee and some salad.

As is the custom on the seven days of mourning, the members of the family were sitting on low stools, with some part of their clothing torn.

I could feel Ben's eyes on me.

I wanted to talk to Ruth's mother alone but he gave me no chance to do that. I don't think he was really watching to see what I did as much as to see who was paying attention to me and why.

Then I thought of a brilliant way to get her alone.

I leaned close to her ear and asked her to please show me the way to the bathroom.

She took me upstairs. They didn't have a fancy house with two bathrooms.

When we got there, I pulled her gently into the bathroom and locked the door.

"Mrs. Schwartz, I don't think, like the police, that Ruth was killed by mistake. I think that someone really murdered her and I want to find out who. Would you please give me your phone number?

I pulled out a pen and paper as I talked to her.

"When I call you tonight, I want you to give me the phone number of any one who was connected with her, friends and relatives. Would you do that, please?"

She nodded and gave me her cell phone number.

I opened the door and she went out. I relocked the door and remained in the room a little while longer while I refreshed my make up. I always eat my lipstick off with whatever I'm eating.

When I came out, there was Ben.

"Oh, do you want to go in? I'm sorry I took so long."

I gave him a big smile and walked past him out the door. He just looked at me and went in the room. Maybe he wasn't following me but it sure felt like it.

I went down and said goodbye to everyone and left the house.

CHAPTER ELEVEN

When I reached home, I was too wired to look at TV so I went on with my tale of woe. This may be my last coherent communication.

==========

My mother hated housework and finally she found a way not to have to do it.

My father didn't have a steady job. He worked for himself – free lance – and made a very good living for us. But my mother used that as an excuse to open a store.

She maintained that his work was too uncertain. That was just an excuse to get out of the house.

She loved being in the store and selling electrical appliances to people.

She wasn't such a good saleswoman because when people bargained with her, she would lower the price.

Then my mother opened another store and my father had to be there all day

My father hated being closed up in a store all day. I remember how, before we had a store, when father had finished a job, we used to be told to pack up some clothes and some food because we were off on a trip to someplace for a few days.

I especially remember going to the Chicago World Exposition this way.

My brother also had to stay in the store after school. I was only 13 and she had to employ a woman to come and do the housework and take care of me.

The first girl she brought was one who had been sterilized because she was a delinquent. This girl used to take me to the park where she met her boyfriend and he would bring a friend for me.

Thank goodness I was too innocent then and all that I permitted the boy to do was kiss me. I had a well developed body and a well developed bust and looked at least 17.

When my mother found out about these meetings she fired the girl and brought an elderly woman to watch over me.

I was what is usually known as a good girl. It was my brother who got into all kinds of trouble.

My father would get angry and want to whip him but I always stood in front of my brother and wouldn't let my father hit him.

I loved my brother dearly.

CHAPTER TWELVE

The next morning I woke quite early. I showered and dressed and then I called Mrs. Schwartz to get the telephone numbers of Ruth's girlfriend, Sara, and Ruth's boyfriend, Ralph.

I called the girlfriend Sara first. I didn't know what to say to her so I told her the truth.

"Sara, my name is Frances Gillian. I don't think that Ruth was killed accidentally, or that I was the intended victim, like the Police say. I think she was murdered on purpose and I'm trying to find out who did it. I thought that maybe you could tell me something about her last few days."

"I don't know if what I can tell you will help," Sara said, "but I'll do anything to help you find out what really happened to Ruth."

"Can I come over and talk to you? Or you can come here."

"You mean now?"

"Yes, if you don't mind. "

"Well I live on Rothschild Boulevard. Where do you live?"

"Where on Rothschild?"

"On the corner of Hashmonayim.

"That's not far from me. Do you want me to come there?"

"Yes, please, I'm not dressed or ready to go out."

"What's your address?"

"The far corner of Rothschild and Hashmonayim. 600 Rothschild, Apt. #r 5. the name on the door is Finkelstein. Alright?

"I'll be there in ten minutes. "I told her.

I picked up my purse, locked the door and dashed down the steps, happy to be doing something that I believed would lead me to a solution of the murder.

Rothschild Boulevard has a park down the center with trees but no lawn or flowers. It's a good place to jog on the packed earth or walk your dog because it's open territory and there would be no danger of getting mugged or raped as there would be in a closed park.

I found the place easily enough and it really was only about ten minutes away.

I rang the bell and the woman who answered shocked me.

She looked like something that usually appears on the cover of a fashion magazine.

Even though she wasn't wearing make-up and her red hair was tangled, she looked good.

Her tangled hair was in the height of today's fashion. I don't know why but everyone was wearing a hairstyle that looked as if you just woke up.

Her skin looked like pink marble, her blue eyes were framed in surprisingly dark brows and lashes. Naturally rosy cheeks and lips, a pert nose and a round chin completed the picture.

"Come in and sit down." She said enthusiastically. "I've seen you on the stage so I feel as though we're acquainted already.

The chair I sat in was more comfortable than it looked.

Her whole apartment was just like her, lovely and bright. When she sat down I noticed that she was a lot stouter than I had thought.

The flowing black, embroidered caftan she was wearing cleverly concealed her girth until she sat.

"Why I came," I began, "I'd like to know what you talked about when you last saw Ruth. By the way, when did you see her last?"

"The evening before she died," she said lowering her head and trying to restrain her tears.

"Why would anyone want to kill Ruthie? She was so good, so kind. When I despaired, she always talked me out of it."

When I looked at Sara, I found it hard to believe that a woman that looked like her could ever despair.

She must have read that in my eyes.

"You think I could never have any problems? Don't kid yourself."

"What did you talk about that day" Was it just before she came to work?"

"Yes. We didn't talk about anything special, just girl talk. She did look worried though and she was so nervous, she couldn't sit still. Wait a minute, I remember a remark she made that I couldn't understand at the time." Sara furrowed her brow.

"What was it?"

"She said: 'There's more in that place than meets the eye.' I thought maybe she was just quoting something from the play. You know she wanted to be an actress, didn't you?"

No, I hadn't known.

"I haven't been there so long myself," I told her. "and this was the first production that I had worked together with Ruth. What do you think she meant?"

"Maybe it was nothing. Just my imagination working overtime."

"And those were her exact words? What had you been talking about just before she said that?"

"About the theater and the redecorating and the rebuilding that was going on."

"Do you know anybody else that she would have confided in? Was she close to any of her family?"

"Not really. They didn't approve of her work and they didn't want her to be an actress."

"Like my parents. I'm sorry we never became friends. We would have had a lot in common. So who would she have confided in?"

"I don't think she was the confiding type. She was a private kind of person. She had a friend called Ralph, but you probably know about him."

"Yes, her mother told me and gave me his telephone number."

"Did she ever mention anyone else in particular. Someone she worked with?"

"Well, there was this man. She never mentioned him by name but she once said that if he was ever found out, he'd be in very deep...ah, you know. I thought at the time that she meant it in a sexual way but now I'm not too sure."

"Was that exactly how she said it?" I asked.

"Yes, although she said he'd be in very deep shit, if you'll excuse the expression.

"That's what I've got to find out. Who that man is. Maybe that's why she was killed because she knew something she shouldn't have known."

"That sounds right to me. Can I help in any way?" she asked.

I thought then that I'd like to have Sara as a friend. I also thought of a way that she might help.

"Why don't you meet me at the cafe in the theater and I'll introduce you to some of the men. I'm sure they would be interested. Wait a minute. Have you ever been there? Does anybody there know you as Ruth's friend?"

"No, let me think. No, I'm sure! When I came to see a show, she would give me a ticket beforehand but we never met there. She was busy after a show so we discussed it here, when she came to visit."

"Okay, are you free tomorrow?"

"From 4:00 until 6:00, I'm free. Will that do?"

"Perfect!"

"Just don't expect me to eat much. I'm on a strict diet. I'm losing weight, I think, in my eyes. You know I feel as if pounds leap on to my frame. It seems that if I sit too close to anyone skinny at a luncheon, the pounds actually leave their hostile host and hurtle toward me and latch on with a sigh and a snuggle, 'Ah, we're home!'"

I laughed...Sara was fun.

I'm very glad to have met you Sara, and I hope we can be friends. I'll be able to get you tickets for the shows I'm in and maybe we can discuss them after wards."

Then I thought of a very important detail.

"Remember, don't tell anyone that you were Ruth's friend."

"I won't, don't worry. I wouldn't want to put myself in danger. Who told you that Ruth and I were friends?

"Her mother. I must call her and tell her not to tell anyone else. Were you ever to her house? Why would she have your telephone number?"

"I can say that she has it because she called me once to pass on a message from one of my friends. This friend lives in a town where Ruth went with the actors to perform. I can say that Ruth called me and wanted to meet me but we never did before she died."

"That's wonderful! You should be a writer with your imagination."

I rose from my chair and Sara accompanied me to the door.

I hate long goodbyes beside the door so I departed quickly.

As I walked home I had this strange feeling in the back of my neck. As if someone was following me. I've never had that before.

Maybe it was because this was the first time I was dealing with a murder.

I ran all the way home, locked my door and took a deep breath.

Stop it, silly, I said to myself.

Anyway the run was good for me.

I called Mrs Schwartz again before I forgot to warn her.

"Mrs. Schwartz," I told her, "I think that Sara can help me to find out who did this terrible thing to Ruth. Sara is a lovely person and said that she will do all she can to help. The thing is, nobody must know that they were friends!'

"Alright," she said. "I haven't told anyone else yet, not even the police. They never asked me about Ruth. They asked me about you. If you had ever been here in my home and if we knew you. I told them that you had never been here before the funeral."

"Good, let's keep it that way. I think I've found out something that may have been the cause of her murder."

"Oh, I hope so, And I hope that whoever did it will pay for it, Miss Gillian."

"Please call me Frances."

"Thank you for what you are doing, Frances."

"I'll call you again if I have any news. Be well, bye."

CHAPTER THIRTEEN

MY FIRST HUSBAND MY SON AND ME

I have most of my day free so I must really sit down and write about my life.

First I have to find the paper I was writing for Ben.

Papers proliferate around here. They disappear and reappear all the time.

Oh, here it is...now I can go on, darn it.

==========

Bringing the family into the USA illegally was what turned our world upside down in 1938 when it was discovered.

At first my mother took my brother and me to Washington where she pleaded our case.

After all, we were a respectable family and had never run foul of the law.

My mother got a very high official to agree to pardon us but our luck ran out when he died before he could sign the papers.

That is when my mother begged me to marry a man I hardly knew to 'save the family' because he was an American.

He was six feet tall, wore heavy glasses, with a potato nose and fuzzy blond hair and was six years older than I was.

I was 2 weeks past my 17th birthday. There was another young man, a much pleasanter one, who wanted to marry me but my mother wanted the older man because he had a car and some money.

Maybe it was for the best as this other young man was killed in the war.

My mother didn't examine the family of the man she wanted me to marry. The father of this man had died of a heart attack in his mistress's bed but I didn't learn about that until much later and my mother hadn't been interested enough to find that out.

Anyway, the marriage didn't solve anything because the authorities said it was a marriage under pressure.

The only thing it did was almost send me to Poland all by myself.

I thought it was a marriage in name only but the asshole had other ideas.

My mother didn't enlighten him. She thought it was a good way to get me off her hands.

I know that was true because this is what she was always trying to do.

She adored my brother.

I was just an impediment.

Maybe there was a little jealousy mixed in, too.

When I married, I didn't even know exactly what went on between a man and a woman.

Only in America could a 17 year old girl be so ignorant.

All my mother would tell me before the wedding is that what a man does to a woman is something she has to suffer and that's it!

That was a lot of help!

He raped me every night. I call it rape when it hurt me because I was dry. He probably had never been with anyone except a prostitute and he knew nothing.

When I complained to the doctor, he said I was just a spoiled brat.

He probably treated his wife the same way.

This was the same doctor who didn't know what trench mouth was and when my firstborn had it and transferred it to my nipples so that it was a torture nursing him, that doctor again said I was just spoiled and sent me home.

I had to stop nursing him at six months while I nursed the others until they were ready to eat.

It seems crazy that I didn't go to another doctor but I was only a naive 19 years old when my baby was born.

I guess I must also have been kind of stupid not to think of doing just that.

I do remember discussing going to another doctor but my dear concerned husband told me I was crazy and that he didn't have the money to waste.

CHAPTER FOURTEEN

While my husband and I were waiting to see what would happen to the family, we had moved into an apartment hotel.

My parents and brother were hiding out in a friend's attic. Just like in "The Diary of Anne Frank.

While I was at home in the apartment hotel, preparing dinner for us, I suddenly got a call from my Uncle Moe, my mother's brother.

"Get out of there immediately, Fran! The Immigration authorities are coming to take you to Ellis Island and then send you to Poland. They think that this way they'll get the whole family.

Ha! My family would have let me go. I was expendable, my brother wasn't.

"They threatened to send me and my wife back to Poland if I didn't tell them where you are, Fran." he cried. "Get out quick!

After the telephone call, I didn't know what to do. I rushed around the room sobbing. I had bought lovely new clothes for my trousseau and I wasn't about to leave them.

I was so naive or is the right word 'stupid?

I had no money, The bastard never left me a cent. I guess he was afraid that I would run away and leave him.

So I took precious time to call my mother-in-law and asked her to wait outside with the money for the cab.

When I threw everything in my suitcase, it wouldn't close and I can still remember myself sitting on the suitcase and trying to lock it and crying my heart out.

I finally got it closed and rushed downstairs. I was afraid that they would stop me at the reception desk but, a miracle happened and they let me go by.

When I reached my mother-in-law's house, I found that I had left my diamond engagement ring and my watch in the apartment.

Then I even had the temerity and perhaps also stupidity to ask my brother-in-law to go there and get them.

At least they didn't stop him and he told me that when he passed the reception desk, there were two men talking to the clerk and he could overhear my name mentioned.

I think this used up the whole allotment of luck that perhaps all of us are doled out in our lifetime.

It certainly was tremendous luck that I wasn't caught then. Going to Poland would have certainly meant death as I was Jewish.

Maybe I had more luck but I just didn't take advantage of it, but that came later.

That's another reason I can't watch a movie or read a book about the concentration camps and what the Nazis did.

When, by chance, as it happened once in the university, I saw a movie about that period, it made me sick to my stomach because it reminded me about that time that I was almost sent back to Poland.

A few years ago, when I went back to Poland to find the place where I had lived. I couldn't even go into more than one of the concentration camps.

When I went into the camp and saw the piles of shoes and eyeglasses, I wanted to vomit. I went out and cried and after that I waited outside while the rest of the group I was with, visited the other camps.

I should be so grateful that I was spared that horrible experience and maybe death.

Here in Israel, we celebrate Holocaust Day by standing still for two minutes in the morning of that day.. The siren blows and everyone stops their vehicle and gets out of the car and stands.

Even the buses stop and everyone stands with head bowed commemorating those who had died.

I stand there and remember how I was almost one of them and how so many of my family died in those camps. My heart hurts as I stand there.

==========

I stopped writing and sat in my room, thinking over what I had written. Maybe after reading this, Ben will understand how hard it is for me to write about my life. Maybe I shouldn't even write about that part of it. Maybe I'm only writing about it to prove to Ben that my life was so terrible. Or do I have another reason to remember all the mistakes I made?

CHAPTER FIFTEEN

After the episode in the hotel apartment, I was hiding out in the attic too! I was afraid that they would send us back to Poland.

A few weeks later, my father went out to the park, he couldn't stand the attic anymore, and said he had to get some fresh air.

He struck up a conversation with a man sitting on the same bench and told him our troubles.

Sometimes you can talk to a stranger about things you wouldn't tell a friend.

To his amazement, the man said:

"No problem! Bring me your passport pictures and $20 each and I'll get you visas to Nicaragua!"

Sounds suspicious, right?

Well, there was no alternative but to hope that he was honest...and he was!

The man brought the visas and we made arrangements to sail to that Central American country that we'd never even heard of before .

We were supposed to leave that week for what is called 'Voluntary Departure' and if we did, then we could all come back in a year.

Sounds wonderful, huh? Too good to be true? It was!

My family was always late for everything and so we missed the boat in New York and had to travel to another state, later in the week, to catch it.

Of course this made us overstay our departure date and we could never come back again to the USA!

The other horror was that my husband insisted that he was coming too!

'You're just going to use me and then throw me away?' he complained.

My family wanted him to come. They probably figured that he might be able to help us return to the USA.

We traveled on a Japanese freighter. It was carrying scrap for the war with China. The captain took passengers primarily to play bridge with him. We played badly but that was fine because he loved winning.

The food was superb. I ate eel wrapped in spinach like a jelly roll and other unusual dishes. It was a pleasant trip except for the time we took on passengers in Texas and couldn't get off the boat because we couldn't reenter the USA. That ship took us to Panama and I can still see that awful looking tarantula spider crossing the street from Colon to Christobel.

In Panama, the two cities were across the street from each other.

Then we took an English boat to Managua, Nicaragua.

I was so seasick on that boat but I don't think it was the journey.

They served us iguana for our meat dishes and I guess my stomach just couldn't take that lizard.

CHAPTER SIXTEEN

OUR HOME IN NICARAGUA

MY FATHER ON A DONKEY IN NICARAGUA

When we reached Nicaragua, I understood why it was so easy to obtain visas to go there.

What a hellhole!

Who in their right minds would want to live there?

You wake up every morning covered with perspiration. There were only about two days in the year when you could wear long cotton sleeves.

There was no air-conditioning in any of the public buildings or, for that matter, in any of the private houses because the climate thinned the blood and air-conditioning would have made everybody sick!

They had a wonderful climate up in their mountain towns. I remember one of them called Leon.

They wouldn't live up there. They would go up in the mountains for a vacation but they stubbornly clung to Managua, a harbor town.

It had a lake filled with alligators.

Once, on a trip over that lake to eat mangos, when our boat was stuck in the middle of the lake, we were lucky that my brother noticed our absence and came to our rescue.

My husband finally left, thank goodness, because the climate was too much for him. He was the kind of man who wore wires under his starched collars, a tiepin and a rubber band attaching his pants to his shirt. He also couldn't get along with my parents.

He was always putting me down and I was too young and too naive to shut him up. All I could do was cry and he never stopped until he made me cry.

When he left, I made the best of it. In Nicaragua, I had my horse, my two big dogs, Kaiser and Diana, (they looked just like their names.) running after me when I rode my horse.

I had a monkey that I made clothes for. He was terrified of the horse and would make in his pants if I held him on my horse.

I had three parrots. A small one, a talking one and a macaw. The one that talked would say: 'Hello, Ralph!'. That was my brother's name. He never said my name which shows you just how far down I was in the food chain of my family.

One night, I woke up in the middle of the night and felt someone breathing on me. I was sleeping alone as my husband had left a few days ago.

I now know what people mean when they say that the hair rose from sheer terror.

Somehow I got out of bed and put on the light.

There, on the pillow, was my little monkey. 'Itchie Scratchie' I called him. He had torn the rope that tied him in his room and escaped and was now lying curled up on my pillow.

I loved the formal balls twice a week. Long dresses and tango music. Boy, could they tango!

The President's palace, where we would go for parties was perched on the tip of a dead volcano. When the president went on a trip, he made all his officers remain on board a ship out in the ocean. Smart fellow but not smart enough. He was assassinated.

We were invited to the palace every week. We played lottery and once I won first and second prizes.

It was embarrassing so I gave the second one away for charity.

Now why can't I have that kind of luck today and win a million in the lottery?

My father had become friends with the president, Samoza, when he started importing cars and had money to give him. He also loved my father's jokes.

When the president met me, he said:

"When your father told me he had a beautiful daughter, I thought he was joking as usual but he wasn't. It's true, you are beautiful!"

Those Latin Americans sure knew how to make a woman feel good.

I once danced with the boy who later became their last president... Tacho.

The women followed our every move and stared with accusing looks. What was a Jewish girl doing dancing with the Catholic son of the president?

I learned Spanish and how to play the guitar. My brother had a tutor but it wasn't considered necessary for me. I just picked it up by talking to the servants and my friends.

CHAPTER SEVENTEEN

I never got used to the two shrunken heads on the wall of our rented house.

The central part of Nicaragua was a jungle and the pygmies who lived there killed their enemies and shrunk their heads. These heads were perfectly formed with their eyes and mouths sewn shut and their hair long and black.

I hated the bats that used to fly in every night. The house was built with space between the roof and all the walls to allow the cooler night air to enter so that made it easy for the bats to fly in freely.

Later my father built himself a house without shrunken heads or gaps where bats could fly in.

I also hated the frequent earthquakes, when we would all rush out of the house with hearts pounding. I also hated the revolutions when we would have to rush home and stay there until they were over.

I think the revolutions were just because the people were bored. They never lasted long. It was only when foreign countries got into the act that they became serious.

The nice part was having servants to do everything and the frequent parties and events. The natives were a proud people. They needed very little to exist. They made a shelter with some banana leaves stretched over some trees, a hammock, two sets of cotton clothes and simple food.

I enjoyed it and perhaps would have stayed there but I couldn't stand my mother nagging me to divorce my husband and marry a rich, old man who wanted to marry me. Again to 'save the family' because we had a hard time of it at first.

My husband wrote to me that he could get me permission to come back to the US after a year in Nicaragua and if I came back to him, I could become an American citizen after a year with him. This time I decided to save myself.

I didn't want to go back to him but I didn't think I could hold out too long with my mother's nagging me to marry that old man. I thought I'd come back to my husband and leave him after I received my citizenship. My wonderful luck or lack of it followed me and I became pregnant before the year was up.

I was 19 when my first son was born. In retrospect, I don't know which was worse, my husband or that old man. All I know is that my husband took full advantage of my being alone and just eighteen.

My father started an importing business very ingeniously. He would put a small deposit down and order a car or an electrical item from the USA that someone wanted to buy and then pay for it after he sold it.

In this way, he earned a lot of money and my parents opened a store that made them very well off. But this took a few years.

==========

Thinking of those first difficult years with my first husband is addling my senses.

Thinking of those years makes me want to do something like breaking dishes.

I guess I'll just go and wash them., I can't afford to break them and besides I'd have to clean up the mess.

I can't go on with this tale.

When I think of those 11 years that I was married to that man I know what people mean when they say they lived a life of quiet desperation. I really don't know what all this has to do with the murder. Anyway, I have to stop and get some sleep.

CHAPTER EIGHTEEN

It was still early, 7:00, when I woke the next morning. (This was getting to be a bad habit.)..I didn't know what to do with myself waking up so early.

I cleaned house (another bad habit), washed some clothes and then I ran over my lines for the next play. I had learned to do that quite cleverly.

I would take a sheet of paper and write down all the cue lines that I had to answer. This would only fill up one sheet.

First, it made the work seem much shorter and it showed me exactly where I was in the play. This made it easier for me to skip around back and forth if some other actor forgot their part.

This came in very handy once or twice.

Now I had another hour free to type some more of my life story.

==========

I came back to my husband and like a fool, I told him why I came back. Now he knew I wouldn't go back to my parents in Nicaragua no matter how he treated me.

At the ripe age of 18, I was stuck in Detroit all alone and he took full advantage of that.

When we went out anywhere, he would always wait until we had no more time and then he would tell me that my hair looked bad and my dress, that I had sewn myself, didn't suit me.

I couldn't understand it because when I arrived at the party, everybody would always compliment me on my dress and on my hair! Why did I let him put me down like that? Now, when I am full of confidence, I wonder why I had so little self esteem.

My husband was full of schemes to make money. Mostly his schemes would entail my working.

First I worked as a department store saleswoman selling lamps and I hated it.

Then, when my first child was six months old, my husband bought a restaurant where I had to wake at 4:00 to go to the market and work all day while a girl took care of my baby.

That wasn't profitable enough so he sold it.

We moved to Lansing when I was pregnant with my second child (The first was not planned. The second was because I didn't want an only child.) We

had a nice synagogue group who did everything together and it was fun.

We took turns making dinner for the whole group and went bowling and played cards and put on shows in the synagogue basement.

My best friend was one of the group who lived in Lansing, and although we were very close, she didn't hesitate to abandon me when I tried to get my money back from my husband. Although he had signed a note that he would return the money that my father had sent me, he didn't return it *and took it away from me and just made out a paper that he would give it to the children when he died.*

Her excuse was that her husband now worked for my husband's company and so she couldn't have anything to do with me.

I remember that once I had my family send her some money as a birthday present because they were so hard up.

I visited her in Michigan and it was sad to see how their health had deteriorated,

He had diabetes and was going blind and she had something wrong with her spine and couldn't stand without holding on to something. I suppose that had a lot to do with her fear of losing her husband's job.

When I acted as a nun in 'Delta Force' and had to cross myself, this dear friend wrote that she had seen me in that movie and she guessed that I would do anything for money. I never wrote to her again. Her son looked me up after she and her husband passed away. A really nice guy.

CHAPTER NINETEEN

After a few years in Lansing, my husband, son and I, pregnant with my second child, all went back to Nicaragua because my father was getting rich there and my husband wanted some of that.

My second son was born there and I almost died from Malaria and a hemorrhage.

I didn't know too much Spanish at the time and when they told me to push, I pushed so hard that I had a hemorrhage.

The hospital there was so primitive. There were open fires under the hot water.

Everybody in the town came to gaze at my son.

My son was born on Christmas Day, was white and Jewish and he had pure white hair and eyebrows and lashes.

Later he became a redhead.

The natives, who were all shades of black and brown brought embroidered dresses for him.

But again, my husband couldn't get along with my parents and we all came back to the USA.

When Pearl Harbor happened, we moved to Washington D.C. where my husband volunteered for a government position since he couldn't join the army because of his eyesight.

Washington D.C. was terrible.

The only places to live there were substandard buildings where the rats were as big as cats.

So we moved to a suburb in College Park, Maryland while my husband worked in Washington.

My third child, my daughter, was born near there in Maryland. She was a surprise as I hadn't planned for another child.

We had a lovely home there. A Japanese man had lived on this street and had planted double cherry blossom trees on both sides of the street. I guess he was lonesome for his country.

Next to the house we had dogwood trees with their beautiful pink blossoms and on the other side, we has a row of tall pine trees.

In the back yard, we installed a swing and other games for the children.

I planted a very successful vegetable garden with corn, tomatoes, carrots, radishes and green onions.

When my daughter was born, my mother sent me one of the girls who had taken care of my son in Nicaragua – Leonora.

We made her a nice room and bath in the basement and she helped me for a year. That was the space of time that she had to stay with me to pay back for my bringing her to America.

I was sorry to see her go but she could make more money working at the Nicaraguan Embassy and she wanted to send some home and I understood that.

CHAPTER TWENTY

MY HOME IN MICHIGAN

The next day, I had an unpleasant surprise. In the mail, there was a note from the police. It stated that the apartment was built illegally and I would have to vacate the apartment within 30 days.

I called the contractor I had bought the apartment from and he said that there was nothing he could do. I called my lawyer and he said the same thing. I asked him why he hadn't told me when I bought the apartment and he examined the contract. He said there had been nothing in the contract that had revealed this information and he was very sorry I was having all this trouble.

That helped a lot. Now I was faced with the possibility that I would lose this apartment.

Also I was informed that my mother was in the hospital in Jerusalem and I decided to drive over and see her.

When I started to drive and tried the brakes, they wouldn't hold so first I drove to a garage nearby.

They told me that my brake was finished and that I would have to have extensive work done on it. I never believe the garages. They're always out to make more money.

I asked him if he had looked at the brake fluid.

The guy looked at me as if I was from another planet and repeated:

"Brake fluid?"

"Yes, please lift the hood and look at the brake fluid container."

Well, seeing that I knew something about it, he had no alternative but to lift the hood and take out the oil container.. Sure enough, it had a leak. There was a hole in the side.

They didn't have a new brake fluid container that I could buy and replace my old one so I went into the kiosk next to the gas station and bought some chewing gum, chewed it for awhile and put on the hole in the brake fluid container.

Then I bought some brake fluid and poured it in and checked the container. It worked. When I had more time, I would look for a new one.

I drove to Jerusalem. In the hospital, my mother told me, in a whisper that she was afraid.

"They're trying to take away some of my organs," she said.

"Don't be silly, mother, "I reassured her. "You're too old to have any organs that would be of any use to them."

She didn't like that answer but she was 86 years old.

"Why did they bring you here in the first place?" I asked her.

"I don't know. I must have fainted because I lost consciousness and the next thing I knew I was in this bed. I think they did something to my heart. Look, they've got a machine attached to where my heart is."

"I'll try to find out from the nurses and the doctor what is going on." I comforted her although I knew that they were notorious for withholding any information.

Surprisingly , they did tell me that my mother had had a heart attack, Luckily it happened while she was in the hospital having her heart checked. I think she must have forgotten that.

She had needed to have a machine attached to her heart but she could go home now if she wanted to. So I took her back to her Senior Citizen's Home.

She had a lovely apartment there. The only trouble was that she was very antisocial and, as a result, very lonely. I used to visit her once a week because she had no one else. I would sit there, sew up her clothes, comb her wigs, and cut her nails.

While I was doing all this she wouldn't stop letting out all her anger on me. Why wasn't I religious?

Once married, a religious woman had to wear a wig or cover her hair. I used to bring her nice wigs from the US.

She found other things to criticize in me. Why didn't I dye my hair. It was going gray and , I thought, looked quite distinguished.

The real reason she was angry was that her life had not turned out the way she had wanted it to. She had everything she needed but she didn't have enough money to buy attention from the grandchildren and great grandchildren to make her feel important.

She was also a worrier. If she didn't have something to worry about in the family, she worried about the government. First the Israeli government worried her and, if not that, then the American government worried her.

I read an article that declared that extensive research had proven that it isn't the parents so much that influence the child, it's the child's peers and environment.

It must be true because I don't worry at all.

I took my mother home and went home myself.

I didn't know what to do about my little apartment. I couldn't sleep and I paced the floor. The neighbors came up to complain that I was making too much noise.

I told them my troubles and they sympathized but also asked me to stop pacing the floor. Which I did.

CHAPTER TWENTY-ONE

After the war, we moved to Wyandotte, Michigan where my brother-in-law owned a newspaper and a radio station.

I worked a little in both. I had an Art Column in the newspaper and a program on the radio, answering people's questions about etiquette.

This was the time I had my first extra-marital affair.

He was my age. It was the first time that I realized that sex could be enjoyable.

We didn't have anyplace to go so we mostly did it in the car.

He wanted to be an actor so we had a lot in common to talk about.

I obtained a place for him on one of the radio programs but he had a bad habit of cursing and one day he cursed when the microphone was open and, to make matters worse, this was just before the next program was announced and it was a church program. Of course he was fired and I never saw him again.

I had saved material for years to build the house of my dreams. I could have drawn the blueprints myself but my husband didn't trust me.

My father sent me the money for the down payment and we built our home.

After it was built, a newspaper, not my brother-in-law's, put pictures of it on the front page of their Home and Garden section.

They called it the house of effortless housekeeping.

It was that!

All the woodwork in the house was natural wood. The walls were washable nylon wallpaper and the floors were nylon tile or wall to wall rugs and heated by inlaid pipes.

It was called radiant heating and ours was one of the first homes to have it installed.

All the closets were walk in closets with windows.

It was one-story with no basement and there were no steps to climb or run down on like I remembered in the other homes I had lived in.

The garage, like the house, was floor heated and it had a bathroom and a drinking fountain (just the low faucet turned up) for the children who played there in the winter.) My son and I made prints of our hands all over the walls. I wanted to print his footprints on the ceiling holding him upside down but my husband wouldn't hear of it. He was such a square!

In the summer I didn't have to give out glasses of water all day, and in the winter they didn't have to take off their boots to go to the bathroom.

A half door connected the garage with the kitchen so I could keep an eye on the children.

My combination kitchen, washroom had a washer, a dryer that had an ultra-violet light in it that made the laundry smell as though it had been in the open air, and an ironing board that folded out and a built in sewing machine.

The kitchen quarters were in the front of the house so I could watch the children if they were playing in front.

This was new in planning a home. As you walked in, the hall had an arched opening and through that you could see a large picture window in the living room, the back of the house and beyond that the woods in the back of the house.

A leather covered metal folding curtain divided the fireplace part from the living room proper so that it made a cozy place for just the family.

It was a beautiful and delightful home but my dear husband could never stand it when I was happy so he made it miserable. He yelled and hit the children if they damaged any little thing.

He found ways to keep me in tears. Even though by now I was 26 years old, he could always make me cry. He wasn't satisfied until he succeeded.

So I left him!

This was the third time.

This time I went to back to Nicaragua. I was really at the end of my rope if I could prefer Nicaragua to my husband.

When I arrived there, I found, to my consternation that only my mother was there.

My mother and father had been on a world tour and had also visited Israel. I wanted to hear all about it.

All that my mother would say was:

"It was interesting."

A few weeks later, I was delighted to see my father. He had returned to Nicaragua even though the doctors had told him that he should not live in that tropical climate. He had returned because he knew that my mother I and didn't get along.

He had Angina Pectoris. At the Mayo clinic, he was told that the climate in Nicaragua was bad for him. Also they didn't have the equipment and the doctors there who could treat him.

He told me all about his trip. He said that if I went to Israel with my children, I could leave them in a Kibbutz (a commune) and go to the city and work and be completely free to do anything I felt like doing.

I didn't quite believe that but I did like the other things he told me about the Kibbutz.

No money was used. Their creed was:

Everyone worked to the best of his ability and everyone received according to his needs.

Of course that's Communism but it wasn't a dictatorship as in Russia..

My father began to feel ill. He had always said that they would find a cure for what was wrong with him and he was right but they found it too late to cure him.

I was sent next to Nicaragua to Costa Rica which had a much better climate.

I was sent to find a residence for my father. I took my younger son with me because he and his brother would always fight and I wouldn't be there to stop it. When I arrived at the airport, I heard my name being paged. Yes, my father had died right after I left. With tears streaming down that I couldn't turn off, I returned.

I decided not to stay in Nicaragua with just my mother.

Oh, how I missed my father all my life. He was the one who would have encouraged me in my career. He would have investigated the man I wanted for my second husband and not just grabbed him as my mother had because she thought that Marvin would be a good worker for her.

That is what my mother did. She always told me that anything she did was for my own good. It wasn't. It was always something she wanted for HER own good, She wasn't lying, she just talked herself into whatever she wanted to believe and really believed it.

I remember once she was talking on the phone and I heard her tell the person that she was sorry that she hadn't been able to keep their appointment because she had felt so bad yesterday.

Then she saw me nearby and realized that I knew she was lying.

When she hung up, she told me that she hadn't felt well yesterday and hadn't told me because she hadn't wanted to worry me.

I hated her lies and told her so. I realized many years later that she wasn't lying, she really believed what she was saying. She could talk herself into anything.

I once worked with a director who was just like her.

After living with my mother and experiencing her manipulations, I could better understand this director.

At that time, my brother was in Mexico, studying at the University.

He was getting married soon and I couldn't go to the wedding.

Not going and enjoying my only brother's wedding was one of the things that I most regretted in my life

I could easily have gone to Mexico where he was being married to a local Jewish girl but just then my son was run over by a car.

Miraculously the only thing that happened to him was that his ear was caught by the back bumper.

Unbelievably, the car had passed over him with his body safely between the wheels!

I was hysterical with the thought that something might have happened to his head behind the ear.

Superstitiously, I believed that if I didn't go to my brother's wedding and immediately returned to the USA and had his head x-rayed, he would be fine.

They had no x-rays in Nicaragua.

So I missed my only brother's wedding.

I was told afterwards that the bride tried to commit suicide because of the way my mother behaved to her!

I could believe that. My mother had an unnatural love for my brother.

My mother even forced the beautiful black haired Rosita to dye her hair blonde.

So I returned to the USA and this time I was determined to leave my husband and find my way to Israel and the Kibbutz.

I took my 3 children and went to New York to find the information I needed, The Kibbutz organization had their offices there.

Meanwhile I stayed with my aunt. She was the wife of Moe, that squealer. She treated us terribly.

This after they had visited us in Maryland and we had given them our master bedroom and taken them to all the sights in Washington.

She wouldn't let the children come into the living room where the Television was.

She took me to the Supermarket right away and told me to buy the food that I needed for the children's meals.

So when my husband came after me and begged me to allow him to come to Israel with us and give him another chance, I agreed.

I think mainly it was to get away from my aunt.

CHAPTER TWENTY-TWO

I couldn't stand writing, remembering and thinking about my first husband so I decided to go on with my investigations.

That afternoon, I talked to the stagehand twins.

The theater was undergoing redecoration then.

They told me that something was not quite right but they couldn't figure out what it was.

"Some of the older actors are acting very nervous. They yell at us for any little thing." said Joe, a veteran in this theater.

"And they have those funny looks. You know what I mean?" said his twin brother, Max.

They were both short stocky men, almost bald and very good-natured.

"You mean like a double take, when a person looks at another person and then quickly looks at him again?" I asked.

"Yeah," Joe said. "and they stop talking, cut off what they're saying, whenever we get too close."

"Yeah," echoed Max. "It ain't what it used to be. That's for sure."

"The few times that I've caught a word here and there, they just seem to be talking about the redecorating. I don't understand why all the secrecy, do you?" Joe asked.

"No, I don't," I said. "But then I'm not one of the 'in' crowd, I don't have tenure so I have to watch my step. You have to be in the theater for four years before you have tenure.

These twin brother stagehands always told me when my part was good or when it wasn't getting it right exactly.

Maybe it was because I always treated them with respect.

It made me feel wonderful when the other actors tried to push me down and someone else knew about what they were doing. Especially, one of the older actors who was always doing bad things to me and my part in a play.

Once I had a very funny part when I was slapped on my backside and I fell each time to the roar of the audience's laughter. This actor went to the director and told him that it wasn't right to slap me on my bottom and to stop it.

The director had to stop that part because he was from England and could have been fired.

Another time, this actor had a very expensive play removed because the reviews praised me and didn't mention him when he was playing the lead!

"Is he one of the nervous people?" I asked eagerly

Because if he was, then I had another good reason to find out what was going on here.

Maybe this would lead to Ruth's murderer.

"Yeah," said Max. "I would even go so far as to say he is the most nervous of all the others, right, Joe?"

"That guy had better watch it, "Joe said. "Cause he's already had one heart attack."

'What about the bar?" I asked. "Which of you is responsible for that bar?"

"The police asked us about that, too, and I feel like shit, cause I should have been the one who tied it. The new guy did it and left." Joe said.

"Did you see anybody going up there or wandering around the steps leading to the bar?"

"No, but it happened when we were on a break and down in the cafeteria drinking coffee."

"So did one of you go up there to examine it after wards?"

"We sure did. Both of us! They came to the cafeteria and called us. We looked at it. It was cut clean like someone had done it on purpose."

"That was no accident. That was out and out plain murder." said Joe. "You were lucky you weren't under it!"

I thanked the two of them and left.

I returned home and I was feeling so good after talking to the stagehands that I decided I could tackle some more of my life story and get it out of my hair.

CHAPTER TWENTY-THREE

My husband and I came to Israel in 1950 with the three children. We would have come sooner, but I wanted to join a communal settlement in Israel and for that you had to train on a farm for a year.

Our training farm was in Vineland, New Jersey.

Our group was called Hashavim which in Hebrew means 'those that returned'. We were called that because we wanted to return to our roots and to the earth as farmers.

There were 19 people in our group, mostly professionals. Among us were a doctor, a nurse, a dentist and an accountant.

I was the driver on the training farm and when I drove the counselors from Israel at 90 miles as hour, they were so frightened that I lost my job as driver.

So I did the laundry, and plucked chickens and scaled fish for the neighboring farms which brought in a little money.

There wasn't enough room in the big building on the training farm so my family was housed in a small two story hut above the chickens.

A blanket separated the children and me and my husband.

The children loved it. I believe that children hate to be alone in their separate rooms.

One night a miracle happened. It was winter and we had a small kerosene stove to warm the room.

For no reason that I can remember, I woke up in the middle of the night. I noticed that the wall in back of the stove was a beautiful rosy color.

For a moment, I looked at it sleepily and almost fell asleep again, when I suddenly sat up and screamed. FIRE!

I woke everyone up and we got ourselves and even the chickens out safely.

The chicken house burned to the ground.

I really don't know why I'm telling all this. Nobody hated me, quite the opposite.

My brother had also come to Israel from Nicaragua with his wife, two children and my mother. They came to go to the city, Tel Aviv and we came to the Kibbutz.

Strangely, they came the same month we came here.

My brother was appointed the Nicaraguan Consul in place of my father who had died.

He could bring in goods without paying taxes.

When I was in the Kibbutz, my mother would bring me lots of goodies, like canned peaches and candies and cakes.

That was food that you couldn't get in Israel at that time.

I would share them with the whole group.

The Israelis that I knew didn't have it in for me either.

The only one who was against me was my husband.

Thinking about him again makes me want to stop writing this.

I'll go and wash some clothes and other tasks.

CHAPTER TWENTY-FOUR

Okay, I'm back. I washed the clothes and hung them out on the roof. I hoped it wouldn't rain before they dried. Then I sat down at the computer again.

==========

On the way to Israel, we stopped off in Italy and saw Pompeii. What an experience! It was eerie walking through that frozen town. I felt as if I were there when it had been a real town and all those people frozen in place by the exploding volcano looked as if they were just sleeping.

We also stopped in Greece and saw all their beautiful ruins.

When we arrived in Israel, we were taken straight from the port of Haifa, on a truck to Kfar Giladi, a kibbutz way up north in the Galilee not very far from Lebanon.

I think the Kibbutz managers were afraid that if we saw the big city we might not want to go to a settlement.

They were excited about immigrants from America. Not many came. They felt that maybe one of our parents or relatives might donate some sorely needed money.

They still think that all American are rich but then, so does the whole world.

My husband and I were given a small wooden hut to live in with no water or bathroom. The communal bathrooms were separate.

The children were taken to the children's houses.

It was so wonderful not to be shut up all day in a house with three fighting and crying young ones. The older son, Howard, 9 years old. The younger son, Marshall, 6 years old and my daughter, Joanna, 3 years old. They would argue and fight all the time.

"Mommy, he hit me!"

"Well, she hit me first."

And I would get so angry and irritated that I would scream at them:

"I don't care who hit first you're all going to get it if you don't stop this!"

It was the only way I could stop the wrangling.

I loved the life in the kibbutz.

I was working in the kitchen scrubbing enormous pots and pans or cleaning the Guest Houses or wiping baby's bottoms but I wasn't alone in the house most of the time cooped up with the three children and a sadistic husband.

I had people to converse with. When I cleaned the rooms and bathrooms, I sang all the time, all the old songs I knew – Night and Day, Jealousy, I've Got You Under My Skin, There Was a Boy, and other songs from the same era.

It was so great coming back to my little shack after work and after a shower with the breeze caressing me.

The surrounding hills of Syria were always inspiring to look at.

In our little hut, there was just enough room for the two sofa beds we had brought with us and and a table and stools.

There wasn't an armchair or a private tea kettle or a private radio in the whole settlement except in the clubhouse.

Nobody even dreamed of having a television set (Ben Gurion, our prime minister, wouldn't allow television for a long time. Oh, was he ever right. The members had to go to the clubhouse to get a cup of tea or listen to the radio.

The children were housed in the children's section where they slept, ate and went to school.

They would come home in the afternoon when we came back from work and we could play with them. It was so wonderful not to have to discipline them or feed them or to dress them. just to enjoy them.

At bedtime, we took them to their beds in the children's rooms, read them a story and kissed them good night.

Then most of us took our guns and went out to stand guard because the Arabs were always stealing our animals and trying to kill us.

From kindergarten the Arab children were taught that it's a great thing to kill an infidel (anyone who was not a Muslim)!

Our dining room was the old stable with not enough room for all. The second shift stood in back of the first shift until they finished eating. This didn't do great things for the digestion of the people on the first shift.

The menu was herring, brown bread and margarine, vegetables and fruits which were market rejects, an egg every other day, a piece of meat or chicken once a week and, if you weren't kosher you could eat more of the meat of the wild boars that they hunted and killed.

I remember that the food was so bad for most of our group that one of our members would shoot cormorant birds, stuff them and cook them.

I love herring and I was glad that there wasn't too much food. I lost weight without dieting!

I was so happy not to be tied down with the children, the housework and my husband.

I worked in the fields, too, but I hurt my back because I tried too hard to keep up with the other workers.

My dear husband pounced on that.

"You're not sick, you're just using this as an excuse not to work," he sneered.

Th nurse and doctor had said otherwise, however, and I knew that I was really ill. I could hardly turn around in bed and I had to walk bent over when I got up out of bed. My husband tried to convince me to leave the kibbutz and go back to America with him. He hated not being completely in control of me.

There was no way I was going to leave this wonderful place and go back to my miserable life with him

He finally took off from the kibbutz, in the middle of the night.

He didn't tell anyone he was leaving. He wanted the management and everyone else to think that I had done something wrong. He didn't realize that, since I had been at rehearsals every evening for the last few weeks everyone knew I had no time to do anything wrong.

We were rehearsing a play by Chechov – 'The Marriage Proposal' in Hebrew!!!

I had asked my husband to attend the rehearsals because it was a good way of learning Hebrew but he couldn't stand the idea of my being someone important.

Although I didn't exactly understand everything I said, it was a great success and we performed it again for the whole district.

After he left, it took me three years to stop shaking when I woke up. This was a legacy from the mornings he used to wake me up screaming that he couldn't find something, that was usually right there under his nose. He just didn't like the idea of me sleeping (although his breakfast was all ready for him) while he had to go to work.

When my husband left the kibbutz, we met again and I gave him permission to use the money that my father had left me to pay the down payment on the new house and that we got back when we sold the house.

So why did I let him have the money? Basic morality, ego and, for all I know, atmospheric pressure but mostly the fear that he might change his mind and stay or maybe return if he couldn't make a go of it in America.

I didn't need the money in the kibbutz.

When I left the kibbutz and moved to the city-(The children didn't want to stay in the kibbutz.)I tried to get my money back. I never got more than a third of it back and I had to pay a lawyer to get that. The other third he willed to the three children but just a little while ago he tried to take it back. In his will, he cheated the children and gave them a small amount, not something that they should have gotten after so many year's interest.

When he left, I could get a divorce. It's not easy to get a divorce in Israel. They try to make you get together and try again and again.

But if the man leaves Israel and leaves his family, that is a good reason to be granted a divorce, thank goodness.

CHAPTER TWENTY-FIVE

MY SECOND HUSBAND

One of the unpleasant things that happened in Kfar Giladi had to do with a group of immigrants who came from India.

They claimed that they were descendants of one of the original tribes who were exiled many years ago from the region.

They called themselves – 'Bnai Moshe' the sons of Moshe.

They were a lovely, gracious group of people, slim, with coffee and milk colored complexions. They were already in the kibbutz when we arrived.

One of the women, who spoke English, told me:

"You know when your group arrived, the kibbutz management took away our new mattresses for your group and gave us old mattresses."

I understood that the kibbutz was very pressed for money. They would receive money from the government for new mattresses and so they saved that money when they switched the old ones. But still it was an insulting thing to do.

The other unpleasant thing was that they tried to separate the people of our group.

We had come with the intention of staying in this kibbutz for a year. (They called this the training year) and then to settle in our own kibbutz.

What the management did was to put some of our people on a different schedule of work and study so that we couldn't meet.

When we complained, one of the members took me aside and explained their actions.

"Look, we want to keep you here. We don't get many groups with doctors, nurses, dentists and other professionals. We need people like you and we'll do everything we can so that you don't want to leave."

But, after the year was up, we left anyway and dispersed all over Israel.

I fell in love with another man in our group, Marvin,

He was directing a Purim play and dancing, singing, and acting in it as I was. I thought what a perfect husband he would make for me with the same interests that I had.

I couldn't have been more wrong. He hated acting and didn't want anything to do with the theater. Much later I discovered that he didn't like to do anything that involved making an effort.

He told me that he got a stomach ache when he appeared on the stage and he didn't need that.

We lived together for a short time and then he told me that he couldn't possibly marry me, a woman with three children.

I understood that and, when our training year, that we were committed to stay in the kibbutz was up, I moved to another kibbutz near a school for teachers and near my mother in Petach Tikva because she was alone when my brother and his family moved back to Mexico.

My father was right and I could have left the children in the kibbutz I was in first, Kfar Giladi.

I didn't want to leave the children all alone all week without a mother or a father and see them only on the week end.

This second kibbutz was very close to the school I enrolled in . I was allowed to study there for three months.

Why do I say allowed? Because that's just what it was. I didn't know it but they had let me come to that kibbutz with my three children because they had their eye on me to take the place of an English teacher who had left.

They showed me the seven classrooms that would have no teacher if I refused to teach them.

There weren't enough English teachers that year – 1951.

Even most of the Americans who were in the country were no help. They had the average 300 word vocabulary, didn't know how to spell and didn't know any grammar.

Most English speaking people can hardly speak or write English anymore. I don't know what they are using but I do know it's not English.

If I had been an English professor, I'd have cut my wrists.

It's not aliens in flying saucers we have to be wary of. It's the slobs of this world. Either they are proliferating or they've always been there, lurking and now they've decided to come out of the closet.

So the supervisor of the school gave me both guns and asked:

"Do you have the heart to ignore all those children? They will not be able to graduate High School. They have to know English in order to graduate.

Me? Would I have the heart. Of course not. He had my number. I didn't want anymore guilt to shlep around.

I felt badly enough about having deprived my children of their father, as horrible as he was, but I felt that was my fault too.

So I taught English. What a load of bricks that was. I wasn't really a qualified English teacher or a qualified teacher of anything!

I did know English grammar however, and was a prize English speller.

Marvin came every two weeks from the Galilee to see me.

That was a 6 hour bus ride each way.

Finally he asked me to marry him. Now that I know him better, I think it was probably because he hated the bus ride he had to suffer in order to come and see me.

I was in love and ecstatic and we were married on the kibbutz in the Galilee, Kfar Giladi.

I should have known what to expect when my new husband, right after the wedding ceremony, instead of staying by my side, went over to his friends to talk to them the rest of the evening.

When girls ask me for advise on how to succeed in married life, I always tell them not to show the men that you love them too much.

They take advantage of you if they see that you are crazy about them.

They can't help it, I guess. Or maybe they want to be the one in control... the one in love...who knows?

I just know that I loved him so much that it actually hurt when he told me that he didn't want to take a walk with me...he wanted to walk alone.

CHAPTER TWENTY-SIX

ME AND MY 3 CHILDREN

"Thinking of Marvin, my second husband and his reasons for marrying me, (One he wanted to leave the kibbutz and two, I had money.)made me feel like I didn't want to go on with my story so just for something to do, I called Ruth's boyfriend Ralph, and asked him if the police had interviewed him yet.

His name was Ralph Houser and he said the police had come and gone already.

"Mr Houser, my name is Frances Gillian. I was standing next to Ruth when the bar fell on her and I want to talk to you about Ruth. I don't believe it was an accident and I don't believe that the bar was meant to fall on me."

"Are you sure?" He asked me. "The reason I ask is that the police were very certain about that."

"Yes, I know what they think but I'm pretty certain too, because I can't seem to think of anybody who would want to kill me. They have me writing my life story so that they can find someone who hates me enough to want to kill me."

"Mr. Houser, some very funny business is going on in my theater and I think that Ruth might have been involved in some way."

"What do you think that something could have been?" he asked.

"I don't really know but I do have some ideas about it. "Maybe she inadvertently stumbled on something that she wasn't supposed to know and was eliminated because they were afraid she might reveal it to the police,"

"What other kind of ideas do you have in mind?"

"Could we meet and discuss this?" I asked him.

"Sure! Tomorrow I have some time free in the evening.

"I'm sorry I can't ask you to come to my apartment because I just moved in not long ago and I'm not settled yet.'

"Oh, that's alright. You can come here. I'm really very interested to hear what you think about the whole situation."

"And I'm very interested in talking to you about it and hearing what Ruth was like and what she wanted to do with her life."

"I'll call you tomorrow before I get home and let you know how to get here, okay?"

"About what time do you think that might be?"

"I usually finish about 5:00."

"Fine! Until tomorrow, then."

I put down the receiver, happy that I was again doing something constructive.

Now all I had to do was finish up my life story so that I could go on full time to find who this murderer was,

CHAPTER TWENTY-SEVEN

Hey, I've got to tell Ben about this. I finally dredged up one person who really hated me. My French cousin, Lillith.

==========

She wasn't really French but Polish.

All her immediate family had perished in the Holocaust.

My British Aunt Leda, my mother's sister, brought her to London and put her in a boarding school. Holidays she spent with Aunt Leda.

In the year of Queen Elizabeth's coronation, Marvin and I finally went on our honeymoon. He didn't want to attend the coronation in London because he said he hated crowds.

I started out alone. First I went to Paris where I bought some lovely clothes. My sister-in-law had loaned me a mink jacket and a white rabbit cape. Now with a gray suit and coat, a gray chiffon short evening dress and lovely accessories that I had purchased, I was ready to meet my very rich relatives in London.

They had diamond mines in Johannesburg, lots of property in England, a private airplane and one of the top dinner clubs in London.

When they saw me, they were stunned.

They had expected a little farm mouse from a backward country.

Israel was only a few year's old at that time and I did do farm labor on the commune where I lived at that time.

My Aunt Leda gave me a room in her sumptuous apartment with another French cousin.

The apartment was stuffed with Victorian furniture, Persian rugs on top of wall to wall carpeting, heavy drapes on curtains and all sorts of little statues, souvenirs, and plants, spread out all over the many side tables.

The day that we arrived, Beatrice, my cousin and I, my Aunt Leda promptly fired her maid and told us to do all the housework.

Well, what did I expect?

She was, after all, my mother's sister and the sister of that snitch, my Uncle Moe.

I discovered that I had another,aunt in England, Aunt Rose. But nobody knew where she was as she had married a gentile and had therefore been ostracized so thoroughly, that they had lost touch with her.

I suppose my Aunt Leda was an imposing looking figure but I think my negative feelings for her made her seem like a harridan.

On the day of the coronation, all the common people were sleeping in the streets in order to save a place at the curb when the queen's carriage and her retinue passed by.

We were sitting comfortably in a flat on Oxford Street where below us, the queen would pass by. This apartment had once belonged to Sarah Churchill.

We watched the parade which was impressive. Leda's son's butler served us goodies while we watched the scene inside the church, the actual coronation of the new queen on television.

It was the first time I had seen Television.

At that time, we had no TV in Israel because our Prime Minister, David Ben Gurion declared that TV was a terrible influence and refused to allow it in Israel.

He was right. We just didn't know it then.

That evening, my husband arrived from Israel and joined us.

We were taken to their prestigious dinner club.

The waiters came over to take our orders. When the waiter asked me if I wanted prunes or shrimp, I ordered shrimp. I didn't realize that he was saying 'prawns' and not prunes. I had to eat the tiny shrimps while the others ate the lovely large prawns.

The waiter brought our dessert on flaming trays.

I am not at all Kosher. Seafood is not Kosher. According to Jewish law, anything that doesn't have certain kinds of legs and scales is not Kosher. Jewish laws seem to make a lot of sense like washing your hands before you eat, and made more sense when there was no refrigeration.

It just seems to me to be very insulting to be a guest who says he can't eat your food because it's unclean. A lot of the food laws seem to me to be very unnecessary now.

We were invited to spend a weekend at their estate near London. The house was really a palace. It was called Grayshot Hall and was the former home of Alfred Lord Tennyson.

Eight bedrooms, a 100 seat theater in the lower floor, and a suite of rooms for the servants that I wished I had.

As soon as we walked in the door, our gracious host, my Aunt Leda's older son began to scream at his wife.

It turned out that she had dared to give the estate cow's milk to the monkeys that they had brought from Johannesburg.

It didn't help when she pleaded that they wouldn't eat or drink anything else!

Our host and I went horseback riding the next morning.

When I commented that with so much land, England could raise her own vegetables which they now imported.

My host looked at me in surprise and said:

"But, my dear, where would we ride?!"

The next day when we returned to London, we were supposed to attend the Derby races.

My husband became very ill and I had to stay with him and miss the fun.

The last day of our visit in England, Lillith, a little girl of fourteen came home from boarding school.

When we were alone, she confided in me how much she hated London and her Aunt Leda.

She asked if she could come to Israel and stay with us on the kibbutz.

I agreed. Little did I know what I was letting myself in for.

First of all, I thought she would be no bother in that kind of community.

Secondly, because I sympathized with how she felt about Aunt Leda. I should have saved my sympathy for Aunt Leda.

Two years later, when we had left the commune and the farm and moved back to Tel Aviv, my cousin from England, arrived to stay with us in Israel.

Now, when I was no longer in the commune and had a small apartment in Tel Aviv, Lillith arrived without any prior notice.

It was very bad timing.

We had hardly any place to keep her but we put her in with my daughter.

Lillith was a female catastrophe.

She disrupted our life. She had a habit of going through everyone's drawers and taking things.

She wouldn't help with anything and we had to clean up after her.

She would flirt with anyone: bus drivers, my older son, my husband, the neighbors and she would absent herself without telling us where she was going and return at all hours of the night.

When I reprimanded her or tried to punish her, she would revile me with terrible words. curse me, and say that I was just jealous of her because she was younger and prettier and she hated me.

I was afraid that she would get into trouble, become pregnant or kidnapped for a slave market.

I decided, together with the social worker, to whom I had appealed, to bring her to live on a commune that specialized in taking care of difficult children.

With that we thought that Lillith was an experience that was finished in a satisfactory way.

We were wrong!

The strangest thing happened.

I perhaps have neglected to say that Lillith was an attractive girl, and knew how to speak French, German and English. She could be very charming when she wanted to and tried.

One day, Lord and Lady Russell visited the kibbutz and met her.

They were so charmed by her that they asked and received permission to take her to live with them in London.

Lillith, in London, became her old self, stealing, dirtying and flirting. When she was punished, she ran away.

When they came to get her, she turned on them with a kitchen knife she had stolen and tried to harm them.

I met Lord and Lady Russell in New York after wards and heard the whole sad story.

Lillith's aunt must have given her money to rent a room in an apartment in Israel, and was paying her expenses.

I met her in a film casting office, a few years later, when she was trying to get a part in a movie.

I know that she wanted to be an actress. She envied me as I was acting in a theater at that time. She was too proud to ask me for help.

After that, I didn't see her for many years but when I went to New York to see one of my relatives who was also related to Lillith, he told me that she is married, and

residing in the US.

He said that she is addicted to drugs.

He wouldn't tell me where she lives...

e wouldn't tell me her married name, Ben, so I'm afraid you'd have a hard time finding her.

Anyway, she doesn't live in Israel anymore and if you think that's a lead, I can give you the address of the relative in New York who is also related to her, and is in touch with her.

CHAPTER TWENTY-EIGHT

Marvin and I went on to finish our honeymoon in America. We sailed from England on the Queen Elisabeth.

What a wonderful trip that was. Dancing and wonderful food and company.

I had all my new clothes and my furs and it was a ball.

In New York we met his parents. They were also astonished to see me. I didn't look like what they thought a woman with three children looked like and I was dressed too elegantly for a field worker resident of a commune.

When I met his mother, I realized why Marvin was so indecisive. When he wanted to take his suit to the cleaners, she objected.

"What are you, crazy? (her favorite phrase) You don't just take one suit to the cleaners. Wait until you have more stuff to take!"

Marvin was always using that favorite phrase on me. "What are you, crazy?"" Until I finally put my foot down and stopped it. But that took a good many years.

After seeing his folks in New York, and attending a few plays, we went to California. Universal Studios had a great show.

We also received some free tickets to a TV dating show pilot that was auditioning. We didn't like it but it went on to become one of the biggest hits on TV and was still on many years later.

Alright, so we weren't experts on what was good or bad!

When we went on to Las Vegas, we were told that there wasn't a single room to be had in the whole town as 4,000 Japanese tourists had just arrived!

Marvin wanted to turn around and go home but I was stubborn, I wanted to see the famous Las Vegas.

So we gambled a little and ate a lot. At that time, you could eat as much as you wanted of steaks and cakes for $1.50!

Then I saw a sign that said that Liberace, the famous pianist was performing at midnight.

So we went to his show which was fabulous, had breakfast and returned to the airport at 4:00 AM.

I fell asleep on a soft divan that they had there then (not anymore) and slept until our flight at 6:00. Marvin couldn't sleep. He was afraid we would miss our flight.

I guess the only reason that Marvin listened to me and did what I wanted in Las

Vegas was because I was supplying all the money.

We went back to England on the SS.Constitution on our way home to Israel. This was another highlight of our journey.

Then we went to Paris where I wanted to see the famous Follies Berger but when Marvin tried to change the dollars we had left, he found that the man had cheated him and taken all our money.

So we went back to Israel as we hadn't enough money left to do anything else.

It didn't help when Marvin told me it was alright because he had already seen the Follies, on his way to Israel.

CHAPTER TWENTY-NINE

MY BRITISH AUNT AND LITTLE LILLITH

When we returned to Israel from our honeymoon, Marvin announced that he wanted to leave the kibbutz and have a farm of his own. He had some romantic notions of life on a farm.

We moved to a co-operative farm in the South where you paid $1,000 and could try it out for a year and if you were dissatisfied with it you could get your money back.

The children and I loved it.

Marvin wasn't happy because he had to get up at night to move the irrigation pipes. The farm didn't bring in any money so I taught school and I had to get up early to go to the next town where the school was situated. Otherwise, Marvin would have made me get up in the middle of the night and move the irrigation pipes, I'm sure.

I still remember fondly, our life on that little farm.

I took care of the chicks after school. Ugh, what bloodthirsty animals they were. When one of them was hurt, all of them would attack it and kill it unless I got there first.

The coyotes came and killed our young goats,

We had a milking cow and shared a horse with a neighbor.

It was great entertainment for all the people in the community when we had to attach the horse to our old car in order to pull it up the hill in front of our house so that we could start the motor going down the hill.

And our cow, well, that's another story.

She was led to the bull and became pregnant.

After awhile, I noticed that her belly had kind of dropped down.

Now in a woman, that's a sign that she will soon give birth so I called the vet and he said that she had plenty of time yet.

I wasn't convinced and I set my clock for 3:AM and, since it was winter, I went to bed with all my clothes on.

My husband laughed at me and made a huge joke of it.

"You think you know better than the vet?" he sneered.

When the clock woke me, I went out to the barn. The cow had given birth and the calf was in the water hole in back of the barn. He could have frozen to death if I hadn't come out to find him.

I shouted the news and the children all got up and brought all my towels to dry him off. Did I ever have a tremendous wash that week.

I never mentioned it again because no man likes to think that his wife is more clever than he is. Especially Marvin. I had to be careful and not notice a sign or anything before he did. It would put him in a terrible mood.

I don't think he ever forgave me for being smarter than the vet.

While we were on the farm, I joined an amateur acting group nearby in Ashkelon.

It met in the evening and I had to drive there on a road that we had been warned was inhabited by Arab terrorists.

I wanted to act so badly that I went anyway.

I was kind of apprehensive, though, when the car was stuck on that lonely coastal road and I had to get out, pull up the hood and suck out whatever was blocking the gas line so the car would start again.

The taste of the gasoline wasn't pleasant but nothing deterred me.

Maybe it was just luck that the terrorists were busy elsewhere.

The boys were doing very badly in school and we didn't know enough Hebrew to help them so I decided to send them to boarding school.

Otherwise I would have had to hire a whole slew of private tutors. Marvin used that as an excuse to decide to leave the farm because he said that he had counted on the boy's help to run the farm.

I'm sure that the real reason was that he hated to get up in the middle of the night and move the irrigation pipes.

We didn't have the computer system for irrigating that they developed later.

So we left the farm and got our cash back!

CHAPTER THIRTY

I'm turning into a Curmudgeon, a real sour specimen. This remembering is souring my adorableness. I could go on and kvetch some more but I think I'll stop. Anyway, it's time to go to bed.

The next morning, my head cleared a little and I sat down at my computer and tried to continue my tale.

==========

After we left the farm, we moved to Tel Aviv, near my mother. She was alone as my brother and his family had left Israel because my mother had made them live in a small village.

She was using them to try and hold on to some property that belonged to some relatives of my father's.

She wouldn't have succeeded anyway because they eventually returned to Israel and reclaimed the property.

Rosita, my brother's wife was very unhappy here. She didn't know Hebrew or much English and she had nobody to talk Spanish to.

My mother refused to babysit the two children so that Rosita could go to the diplomatic affairs to which my brother was invited.

My mother maintained that she was the one who should accompany my brother to those affairs as her husband had been appointed the Nicaraguan consul to Israel before he died.

When we left the farm, I began to teach English to adults and I joined a little theater in Tel Aviv.

The way I gained admittance to the group is a way I would recommend to any wannabe actors.

I had studied commercial art and graphics in High School and knew how to sew and paint so I could draw letters and make a good-looking sign. But this method would work with being a dresser or an assistant director.

I just marched into the theater and told them that their window looked terrible. It really did. Of course their answer was:

"Can you do better?"

And my answer was:

'Of course!" And I did.

For awhile, I just made props and sewed and painted scenery and was general gofer which means go for this and that.

I have always told wannabe actors who come to me for advice on how to get into a theater, to be close to the theater in any way they can even as a gofer.

When an actor is needed and they want to hold an audition, they will first look around to people close by. This is because they don't really want to go through the hassle of block long lines of people and all the time wasted auditioning them.

I got the part originally, only because they were trying to force someone else to do it.

It was the role of the Widow Quinn in 'The Playboy of the Western World' by J. Wellington Synge.

The other woman didn't want it because it was the part of an older woman.

The director gave me the part because he didn't think I would ever be able to do it as I didn't know enough Hebrew. He was sure that the other woman would eventually have to take the part to save the show.

I ended up performing and walking off with the best reviews from the critics

I was 38 years old now, much older than anyone else in the group,

When I told the director that I could be like a mother to them, he quipped:

"Do you want us all to develop Oedipus complexes?

True, I only looked about twenty five.

I played another leading role but not so well and so I decided that I needed some education in acting.

Therefore, I enrolled in the first Drama faculty of the Hebrew University.

Everything went very well until the middle of the second year when the teacher, for no reason that I could see, suddenly attacked me verbally so strongly that I felt I had to leave.

When I first came to that class, this same teacher had announced that I was a born actress.

So then I joined a studio and the teacher, I think he was a frustrated actor who became a director, also treated me very badly. This director hated the idea that I could speak Hebrew with a good accent and he couldn't do it. So he took every opportunity to belittle me.

Looking back on it, I realize that I was probably over-sensitive. But how can you be a good actress and not be sensitive?

At this time, a friend and I founded *The Little English Theater in the Z.O.A. House in Tel Aviv.*

For the first production, he and I did 'The Fourposter'.

The most important critic in the country - Dr. Gumzu reviewed it and called it 'definitely West End standard". He also praised my performance but he got my name wrong.

When I asked my teacher what he had thought of it, all my wonderful drama teacher could say was:

"You don't want to hear what I thought of it."

CHAPTER THIRTY-ONE

PAUL NEWMAN AND ME IN 'EXODUS'

I didn't wake up until 10 the next morning (Good I'm getting back on track) and I had to hurry to get to the theater at 11:00 to meet Sara,

She was sitting at a table and talking to a man at the next table.

He was the actor that was giving me all the trouble and he was the one that was acting the most suspicious.

I said hello and sat down. He left.

I asked Sara how she had happened to start up a conversation with just that man?

"Well, I was kind of just looking around and he asked me if he could help me.

I said: "No thanks, I was just waiting for you."

"But he kept on talking to you didn't he? How long have you been here?"

"About 15 minutes. He asked so many questions about you."

"He did, huh...what for instance?"

"Well, did you ever tell me your future plans and what your most secret wish was. I told him we hadn't been friends long enough and I didn't know you too well."

"Which is the truth."

"But he kept on talking. He asked if I had known Ruth and I said Ruth who?"

"Good for you."

"And he told me about the tragedy...in quite some detail."

"He was backstage that day, you know."

"Really? And you think that he...?"

"Shh, let's not talk about it here. What would you like to drink or eat."

"Just a glass of fruit juice. It's too early for lunch.

"I'm hungry enough to eat a horse!"

"Sorry, no horse on the menu today!"

"Then I'll settle for apple juice."

"Did you ever notice how much it resembles urine?"

I laughed. "Ooooh, I need you around me. With remarks like that, I'd lose my appetite."

"I wish I could lose mine."

I went to the counter and brought back orange juice.

"Did you ever think of becoming an actress," I asked her.

"With my figure? I think the fates are punishing me for being so arrogantly slim when I was younger."

"You're very attractive and you have a lovely speaking voice. Maybe that would give you the motivation for losing weight."

"Oh, there's something else you should know about me. I can't memorize. Words do not come at my bidding. They seem to jam up on the way from my brain to my mouth. They're still mine to enjoy but they refuse to exit!"

I couldn't stop laughing. We finished our drinks and I suggested that I show her the backstage and our dressing rooms. That was so that she'd know what I was talking about when we discussed the theater.

After that, we made a date to see each other next week.

She asked me to have lunch at her house.

I accepted because, as I told her, I knew I wouldn't have to worry about a big, fat meal.

That was also a hint that I hope she caught.

CHAPTER THIRTY-TWO

One of the nice things that happened to me when we reached home from our honeymoon, was my receiving a part in the movie 'Exodus'.

Even that was tainted by people trying to undermine me.

When I heard that they were asking for actresses for the movie, I put on a house dress, tied my hair in a kerchief and left off my make-up.

I've always maintained from what I've read, that movie directors need to see the character dressed and looking like what they need to be in the movie.

So I dressed like an immigrant and got the part, head of all the women on the boat that was coming from Cyprus to Israel.

All the people who escaped from Europe and Hitler, had been interned in Cyprus when they tried to enter Israel.

In the film, we sailed from Cyprus to Israel (it was still Palestine then) and the British wouldn't let us land so we all went on a hunger strike.

In the film, I had two children. My part was telling Paul Newman (the captain of the boat) off. He wanted to stop the hunger strike by sending the children back to Cyprus.

My scene with him was up on the bridge with my two children and another woman with her baby.

"You know nothing"I told him, "My children were born behind barbed wire and not you or the English are ever going to put them back there again."

Of course the scene was shot separately with first Paul and then me on camera.

He was such a wonderful person that even though he didn't need to stand there when I was talking to him, he asked me if it would make it easier for me if he stood there.

When we rehearsed the scene I noticed that the children weren't the same as those in my last scene and I mentioned this to the director. Otto Preminger.

He scowled at me and said:

"What's the matter, aren't these children good enough for you?"

When I explained that I thought it would be bad for continuity, he blew his cool and got the original children back. I was so flustered that I didn't want to tell him that the clothes on the children weren't the same as before. I should have told him.

When I saw the movie, I saw that they had cut out the first scene that showed me walking up the steps to the captain's cabin, and I'm sure the clothes not being the same was the reason.

When Preminger heard what they were paying me, he gave me a thousand dollar bonus!

The Israeli director wasn't acting mean to me because he disliked me. He was trying to obtain this part for another woman whose father was an important director in a theater and could help him in his career and he also could siphon off some money for himself.

Everybody was a little afraid of Preminger. One day, when he passed by and saw me talking to a handsome cameraman, we both froze as we saw him.

He turned the corner and then stuck his head back in and said:

"Please, not to seduce mine actresses!"

I remember a crowd scene when the Israeli flag was raised for the first time and he shouted through his megaphone:

"Everybody, do what Zipora is doing!" Zipora is my Hebrew name.

Another day, He took me aside to talk to me.

"Are you happy in Israel?" He asked me.

I should have said:

"No, I would like to come to Hollywood!" but what would I have done with my three children? I didn't want to take them away from Israel and I couldn't leave them with my mother. Not with her philosophy.

So I said that I was very happy in Israel and lost a wonderful opportunity.

Looking back I can realize how stupid I had been.

I didn't know that in Israel, you couldn't become famous if you didn't become that in another country.

As it was, two of my children, the older boy and the girl, later left Israel and went back to the USA.

CHAPTER THIRTY-THREE

The next year, I had to return to the US for a year because I wasn't native born. This was according to the McCarron Act where naturalized citizens had to return every five years and live in the US for a year. It was repealed a year later.

One month after I left Israel and returned to the US, the American government ordered all American citizens to leave Israel as the Suez War had just erupted.

So I wrote to my mother and asked her to send me the children.

My mother sent me back a paper that would have given her complete control of my children.

By this time, I knew enough not to trust my mother and so I sent her back a paper only giving her the authority to send me the children.

She sent me my youngest, Joanna, who had been studying ballet at a school in Tunbridge Wells in England for the last three years and usually came back to Israel for her summer vacation and now she came to us in the US for the summer.

My youngest son was sent to live with his father in Michigan. He has returned to Israel and had no connection with his father since then so I suppose it wasn't a pleasant experience. He won't say much about it.

The older boy refused to leave Israel,

In America, in New York, I found an Off-Broadway theater on Second Avenue that had a terrible show window and I used the same shtick I had used in Israel to worm my way into it.

I did Graphics there, making signs and decorating, sewing and painting, and was stage manager in the morning rehearsals and in the evening performances.

In between I worked the lunch hour on Madison Avenue to make money to support myself as my husband refused to help me.

When this theater had auditions for a Pirandello play, I tried out and got the part.

I gave that up for another part in another theater where I was paid.

Then, without even asking for an appointment, I marched into the office of the most important agent in New York, William Morris, and told him, no less, that I wanted him to be my agent.

Sometimes, I look back in wonder at my hootzpa, my nerve!

He looked at me disdainfully and remarked.

"Who said you're an actress?"

I just stood there and didn't know what to say.

At that moment, like in a dream sequence, a man came in from the lobby where the door connecting the lobby was open and said:

"Mr. Morris, you're going to think that this is a setup but honestly, I don't know this woman but I saw her in a production in an Off Broadway theater last night and she stopped the show!"

It was true. I had performed in a bad play and the audience had applauded after my scene.

I was playing a woman prizefighter, if you can believe it.

Of course the fight scenes were faked but with cotton in my nose and mouth, I looked the part. I confirmed his statement.

Mr. Morris looked us over and then said:

You're either telling the truth or you're a very good actress. I'll take a chance on you!"

He sent me to do a part in a live TV show and I did it so well that they gave me an Aftra card. This was the TV Union card.

It was and still is a Catch 22 card.

You had to play in a TV show to get the card and you had to have the card to play in a TV show.

I didn't realize at the time what a great gift I had been granted.

Then I went to take part in a summer stock theater. You had to pay in order to get into a Union theater and I didn't have the money.

I was very successful in the parts I did there and even sang in the leading role of the musical 'The Boyfriend'. I can't sing but I holler real good! I also got terrific reviews in the play "The Glass Menagerie'.

When the year was up, I went back to say goodbye to Mr. Morris.

When I told Mr. Morris that I was returning to Israel he told me that I was crazy to leave the USA. I had the promise of a good career here.

I should have stayed in New York and made a name for myself.

I didn't realize at the time how much that would have helped my career in Israel.

But that would have meant either having my children brought up by my mother in Israel or bringing them to New York.

Neither of those solutions could wipe out a feeling of guilt.

I didn't want my children brought up in the US, with all the drugs especially in New York or brought up by my mother.

When I returned to Israel, my mother asked one little favor from me. That I not work with that little theater group anymore.

She probably thought that no other theater would have me and so she'd have her little servant back.

After all, I used to fix her hair and nails and iron her clothes and go shopping for our food and talk to the contractors and drive her around.

She would get angry at a tradesman and send me to smooth things over.

I thought that giving up that theater was very little to do to make her feel better but that was a mistake.

I worked in another commercial production in another theatre where I took the part of the Lesbian in 'No Exit' by Jean Paul Sartre. I was very good in that part.

I was promised the lead in their next production but it was given to another actress.

That hurt me very much and I felt very sorry for myself until someone told me:

"Don't take it personally...people step on you not because it's you but because you're in the way when they want to get some place."

CHAPTER THIRTY-FOUR

That evening, about an hour before the performance that I came to see,I went backstage to see if I could talk to the man who had been in charge of the flies and the bar that had killed Ruth.

No luck. He had been fired. When I asked one of the workmen who fired him, he told me that Sam had done it.

Sam was the actor who had been talking to Sara and the one who always made trouble for me.

He was also the one that the stagehands said was looking so nervous.

I could imagine him murdering someone, but why?

That was the catch.

If it was blackmail, what could she have been blackmailing him about?

The next morning, I went to another garage to fix my brake oil canister.

The man in this garage looked at my old brake canister and said the hole was too big to fix.

"It looks as if someone doesn't like you, miss."

"Why?"

"That hole is handmade and fresh, too."

"You can tell all that just by looking at it?"

"I've been in this here business more years than you lived, miss. I can tell!"

That was something to think about. Should I tell Ben? Then I'd have to tell him what I've been doing and I didn't want to do that yet.

I felt kind of sick thinking that someone wanted to cause me to have an accident and perhaps even lose my life.

Maybe Ben was right and that bar was really meant to fall on me.

Or was this happening because I was meddling in something I shouldn't be meddling in.

So I bought a new canister, paid the garage man to install it and drove home.

The next day I was going to see Ralph so I figured I ought to take a nap and get some beauty sleep.

It took me a long time to fall asleep.

I usually read a few pages of a Hebrew book and that put me to sleep.

The effort of concentrating on a foreign language, seems to cut off the things I've been thinking about all day and I become drowsy and fall asleep.

Okay! I made it. Only 20 minutes. Just right. Too long a map makes you feel groggy.

It's funny, they tell you not to nap if you want to sleep well at night but I sleep better if I've had a short nap that day.

Alright, so I'm weird, I've never denied it.

CHAPTER THIRTY-FIVE

THE TAMING OF THE SHREW

TOPOL AND ME - IN
THE TAMING OF THE SHREW

A CARTOON OF ME AND TOPOL IN

'TAMING OF THE SHREW'

A CARTOON OF ME

It was then that I heard that a new theater was going to be opened in Haifa.

So what did I do?

I saw the director sitting in a cafe and I went up to him and asked for an audition.

After the audition, he praised me and said I was a mixture of the two leading actresses in Israel. He gave me the leading part in the first production - 'The Taming of the Shrew ' by Shakespeare.

I couldn't possibly guess that this would be the nightmare that it turned out to be!

I didn't know that the woman he hired to do the make-up and the dressmaking were both ready to do anything and everything to make us fail because they didn't want this theater to succeed.

So who did they attack? Me, the weakest link.

I wasn't expert in Hebrew yet and I was so busy learning the part that I didn't pay attention to anything else.

In those days, the first night was critic's night, now they allow nine days to run the show before the critics come to review the play.

Opening night, the make-up woman made me up so badly and fixed my wig so queerly that the reviewers even commented on it.

The dressmaker left uncut material in the dresses to make me look fat.

Our famous scenic designer, Theo Otto, made me the one dress that looked good on me.

I looked so bad that one of the critics wrote:

"Frances always looked so good but not this time. It must have been the lighting."

More important, my partner, who played Petruchio, liked to trip up other actors, he maintains that it's all in fun!

The result was that I almost failed in the part.

He would try to confuse me by talking to me in such a way that only I heard him. He knew I wasn't an expert in the Hebrew language yet.

Then he would try to tickle me. It angered him that I wasn't ticklish.

He told me that I smelled bad. You can imagine how that made me feel.

There was another actor in the play who got good notices. While this actor was playing, my Petruchio kept whispering to me not to look at this actor or pay attention to him. I always concentrated on whoever was talking or doing any action onstage.

This is what I was taught to do and this is good manners and good ethics but that wasn't on the menu for my partner.

This is when I realized what kind of terrible person he was.

Katherine, the Shrew couldn't be a shrew if the other actors didn't react to her but they all didn't , they ignored me. I can imagine who put them up to it.

Even , one evening, when my leading man had a blackout, I was the only one to jump in and save the situation. The others wouldn't do it because it would have made them look as if they had forgotten their lines.

I, like a fool, thought that it was enough to love the theater and do everything you could for the performance and for the audience.

When we were doing 'The Caucasian Chalk Circle, he was the lead and I had a scene as an old lady and everyone said it was a wonderful scene. He had it taken out as he said it didn't do anything for him. Just showed him up, I think.

I had the same leading man playing my husband in Brendan Behan's play 'The Hostage'.

For the two months of rehearsal, he wouldn't talk above a whisper, he said he was feeling out the part.

Opening night, he changed all the blocking and became the aggressor when he should have been the humble husband. He also spilled real beer all over me.

He insisted on it being real.

One evening, when I was sitting at the table with my head bowed, he spilled bear on my head. I stood up with my full beer mug in my hand, He knew what I was going to do and he said:

"Hey don't you know that beer is good for your hair?"

I threw my beer right in his face. It was in the spirit of the play for me to do this, I would never do anything, no matter how I felt, not in the spirit of the play.

The worst was when one evening, I mispronounced a word.

The audience wouldn't even have noticed it but my leading man walked downstage and repeated my mistake to the audience several times so that they would notice it. He was a horrible person.

I think the trauma of that incident stayed with me all the rest of the years and kept me from doing as good work as I could have done.

In one of the plays, I later performed in, I pronounced a word wrong and couldn't get it right again and it was very embarrassing. That theater never asked me to perform there again.

I cursed him once, saying that I hoped that he would someday have to perform in a foreign language and he would fail!

He did fail. He failed in Othello and the critics said it was 'Othello with out Othello'. He played the leading role in the film 'Galileo and critics wrote that any of the other actors in the film could have done it better.

He participated in other films but wasn't successful. One of his critics wrote that he should learn that it wasn't enough just to make faces .

He was only good in 'Fiddler on the Roof' and I hear he's still doing only that play now.

He even tried making a film by himself but it was so bad that it only lasted three days.

In the next season, in Haifa, our director gave us, the original troupe, only small parts and invited other actors from other theaters to do the leads.

We, the actors, said we would leave if he continued to do this.

I was the only one to leave!

CHAPTER THIRTY-SIX

Just then the phone rang and Ralph, Ruth's boyfriend said that he was home and I could come over whenever I wanted. I said that it would take me an hour to get ready and he agreed.

He lived quite a distance from me in Jaffa so I took the car. I hoped I'd find a place to park. As I drove to Ralph's place, I kept looking in the mirror to see if anyone was following me. I felt uneasy.

I did find a parking lot but I still had quite a distance to walk. I don't mind walking but this was through a lot of dark narrow streets.

Jaffa had been rebuilt but the old part of town had kept its style. It was a lovely place to visit in the daytime but not so nice alone, at night.

It's situated on the shore of the Mediterranean Sea. Wide spaces and two story dwellings and stores all built together and presenting a solid wall although not ruler straight, of rectangular stones. The dwellings had lovely patios inside.

They reminded me of Nicaragua where all you could see on the street were walls with doors but when you opened a door, there was usually a lovely garden with all the rooms opening out on it. It would be too hard to heat a home like that built of stone,but who had to worry about heating in Nicaragua?

I had no trouble finding his apartment. They were once Arab buildings and beautifully built with arched windows and doors. In the inner walls.

Ralph brought me in through a small courtyard into the living room, asked me to please be seated and excused himself, saying:

"I'll be right back."

I caught a fleeting glance of a dark-haired, tall man before he fled.

As I entered, I could see that Ralph had left it pretty much in its natural state.

The floor was covered with the original Arabesque tiles. Unlike our monotone tile coverings, these are arranged to look like a carpet and are lovely to behold.

The large living room had arched windows and a very high ceiling. The walls were very thick and this created window seats beneath the windows that looked out on the courtyard. These were padded with pillows covered with Oriental embroidery.

The furniture was unmatched old pieces that he had probably picked up in the Flea Market here in Jaffa.

A large brass tray beautifully carved on folding legs served as a coffee table.

The sofa and occasional chairs were all carved and upholstered in bright velvets. A very large trunk with brass fittings had a few lovely plants and carving on it.

A carved buffet also had some plants and photos on it.

I saw a large photo of Ruth in an elaborate frame. Strangely enough, she was made up to look very exotic. Then I remembered Sara telling me that Ruth had wanted to be an actress. Perhaps this was one of her publicity or resume photos.

The hangings on the walls were some oriental carpets and some lovely watercolors. I was looking close up at one of them, of the port in Jaffa, when Ralph returned.

"is this your own work, Ralph?"

"Oh, I'm just an amateur painter."

"You're too modest. Did you also decorate your home all by yourself?"

He nodded.

"I like what you did very much."

"Thank you."

While we chatted about how and where he had bought certain pieces and how much or rather how little he had paid for them, I had a chance to really look at him.

He was older than my first impression. There was some gray in his sideburns.

His eyes were also gray and unusual in their size, almost hypnotic I would say. His skin was slightly olive in color and his facial features were masculine.

A bold nose, sculptured lips, high cheekbones and a heavy jaw. The jaw was what saved his face from being too handsome.

He must have been a lot older than Ruth but I could see that he would have no trouble attracting a woman. I was attracted and felt it a little.

It was getting late and I wanted to talk about Ruth.

"The reason I came," I said, "was that I wanted to learn more about Ruth."

"Poor Ruth. She was just in the wrong place at the wrong time, wasn't she?"

"No, I don't think what the police think, that she was killed by accident. I told you that over the phone, remember?"

"Yes, you did. The police, however, convinced me otherwise. They were certain that you were the one slated to be murdered."

"I know. The detective in charge has me spending my days writing the story of my life so that he can find someone who hated me enough to try to kill me."

"I can't imagine anyone hating you that much," Jack smiled at me. He was charming on top of being so attractive.

'Well, maybe it wasn't that. I think that Ruth was killed because she knew something that could harm someone. Did she ever talk to you about the theater?"

Oh, lots! That was what we had in common!"

Oh, are you connected to the theater, too?"

"I wish. No, I had to make a living at a very early age so I had to be practical. I'm a businessman. I deal in whatever will bring in money. Real estate, insurance, investments and things like that."

"How did you meet Ruth?"

"You are perhaps implying 'what in the world did we have in common', right?

"Well, yes, I was thinking of that, too."

"I met Ruth at a party a producer friend of mine was giving. We started to talk about the theater and never stopped. It is a subject that fascinates me. I wish I had had the time and the opportunity to be an actor. Maybe I'll be a producer one of these days if I ever make enough money."

"You would have made a fine actor," I said blushing. "What did Ruth tell you about her work in this theater/ She hadn't been there more than a few months. Did she relate any gossip to you?"

"She had a lot to say about everybody there. She liked you. She said you were very professional and polite to everyone.

"Can you recall anything she said that might throw some light on why she was killed?"

He was silent for awhile and seemed to be trying to think.

"I've been turning that over in my mind since you called. I can only tell you that she was planning on going soon to England or America to enroll in one of the academies or studios for actors. When I commented that this would necessitate a lot of money, she just looked at me and smiled a mysterious smile.

I didn't want to tell Ralph that I thought she was into blackmail. I wanted to hear what he thought she was doing.

"That seems strange to me. Where would she get it from?" I asked, trying to look innocent.

"Well." he said, "she was determined. She spent all her money on lessons or saved it by not buying clothes or makeup. She studied dancing and voice, Tai Chi and fencing, Transcendental Meditation and things like that."

"Transcendental Meditation! I'm a teacher of that. I could have saved her by teaching her for nothing. All that Indian mumbo jumbo that they add isn't necessary. Paying for it is necessary for some people because otherwise they wouldn't believe or persist in it."

"I took some of the lessons together with her," he told me. "The Tai Chi and fencing and Meditation. You know, I feel much better since I started those lessons, more in control of myself."

"I do too, "I told him. "I used to have an uncontrollable temper but now I can control it and also it takes away some of my pain when I have it."

"A very famous American writer, Kurt Vonnegut wrote in an article:

"Lately, it's very boring around the house. Since my daughter and my wife have started doing Transcendental Meditation, they don't get pissed off any more."

Ralph laughed. "So it's not just us. Do you go to any of their meetings?"

'NO!" I almost shouted and Ralph recoiled as if I had pushed him.

"Hey, just because I can control my temper doesn't mean that I've lost any of my temperament. If that happened, I'd have to stop being an actress."

"So why are you so opposed to going to their meetings, Frances?"

"Because I don't need to and because I think all that is the commercial side of T.M. I hate that."

"Well, being a business man, I can appreciate that side of it."

I looked at my watch. It was close to midnight.

"Ooo, it's getting late. I've enjoyed our talk so much that I didn't even realize how late it was becoming. You're easy and pleasant to converse with. I'll bet Ruth liked talking to you, too. I think that what you have told me just strengthens my belief that Ruth really was intentially murdered. Now I think I know the why of it but I still don't know who, although I have my suspicions,"

"Aren't you afraid for you own life if you find out too much?"

"A little. I'm very careful, though. By the way, does anyone besides Mrs. Schwartz know that you were Ruth's friend?"

"I don't think so. I attended many of the plays in the theater but Ruth was busy after the show so we met other times and discussed the plays. But the police know I was her friend."

"Good, let's keep it that way. Don't acknowledge me if you happen to accidentally see me in the theater."

"Alright, if you want it that way but I hope you have no objections to my seeing you other times and other places."

"For now, I think we better just meet here. We might be seen by the wrong person if we went out anywhere. I hope you understand."

"Well, then, please come to dinner this Friday, would you?"

Somehow I didn't feel right letting him make a dinner for me.

"I will if you let me bring the dinner. I'll get a roast chicken and some wine, alright?"

Alright, but I think I'm getting the best of the deal. As soon as all this is all over, I'll treat you to the best restaurant in town."

"I'll enjoy that."

"And now, let me take you to your car so that I'm sure nothing happens to you on the way."

"You don't have to do that but I must confess that I'd welcome your company. This neighborhood doesn't spend too much money on lighting."

"That's to keep the ambiance of an ancient, small town."

Ralph helped me put on my jacket and then put on his, too. It was much faster going back to the car because now I knew where I was going. Ralph looked at my little white Fiat with appreciation. I was glad that I had it washed a few days ago.

"Meeting you, Frances, is the only good thing that has come out of this incident."

What a nice thing to say.

"Thank you," I said. "I feel the same way."

Ralph lightly pressed the hand I held out to him. I was glad he didn't try to kiss my hand or me as others have done when I first met them.

I drove back home and then ran to the entrance of my building and up my steps and closed the door of my flat with a sigh of relief.

As I fell asleep, I let my mind embroider a few fanciful ideas.

CHAPTER THIRTY-SEVEN

I was going to see Ben later in the day so I figured I better get busy and write some more of my life. When was I going to finish it? It seemed like there was no end to it. Now I'll give Ben another slice of my bad luck.

THE MOTHER IN
'THE GLASS MENAGERIE'

I had performed 'The Glass Menagerie' by Tennessee Williams in America, in summer stock in the year that I was there. The critics wrote reviews comparing me favorably with the original Amanda in the New York Broadway production. If you want a copy of the review, I can give you one. I have about 50 of them,

I came to a theater in Beersheva, the southern part of Israel, and suggested to the Artistic Director who was also the boss in that theater, that we do 'The Glass Menagerie'. To my surprise and joy, he agreed and said that we would go into rehearsal as soon as I was ready!

So I moved to that city and started to work. After two weeks, my director told me that she didn't want to work with me in the part anymore as I was already what she wanted me to be.

That was wonderful to hear. Everybody was very excited after seeing the general dress rehearsal,

Then the director of the theater called me in to his office and broke the terrible news. We couldn't do the show as another person had the rights and absolutely refused to let us have them. There was nothing to be done. We had to close that show.

I went on to play in that theater. I had some good roles but nothing like 'The Glass Menagerie.

It's trauma time, Ben, I'm hoping the rest of my life will turn out better.

Apropo or maybe not, the gentleman who had the rights and refused to give them to us, was a man I once refused to have an affair with. I'm sure he doesn't hate me enough to kill me. He has already found an original and devastating way to take his revenge.

Some of the good roles that I did in Beersheva were – The mother in 'the House of Bernarda Alba', 'Entertaining Mr. Sloan' and 'The Subject was Roses'.

The downside was that in the many years that I was there, I came down with Bronchitis every opening night. This continued until my daughter, Joanna, came to visit me. She had been working in a theater in New York when she was invited by a theater in Israel to play Clytemnestra in the a Greek play, Agamemnon, all expenses paid.

Steven Bergof came from England to direct it and my daughter walked off with all the best reviews.

When she came and saw me, I was really in a bad shape. My tongue was burning, I had cracks in the corner of my nose and mouth, my eyes were over sensitive to the stage lights, The skin on my face looked like the skin of a turtle, and I had to pack myself with cotton because every time I laughed or screamed, I literally peed in my pants.

I had seen all the doctors about my urinary problem and there were some good ones in the University and the famous hospitals there. They all said that nothing could be done as I had ruined my bladder muscles by not urinating when I had to and holding it in too long. They said I should have gone to the bathroom every three hours whether I had needed it or not.

When my daughter saw me, she immediately announced that I had a classic case of vitamin deficiency.

She was an amateur nutritionist and read all the books.

So I began to read up on the subject and what I read really opened my eyes.

I began to do every thing by the book – a book by Adele Davis. She prescribed a drink that had everything in it. I took it for four months before it rid me of all my troubles and changed my life. Everything that I had wrong with me vanished! My sensitive eyes, the cracks in my face, my burning tongue, my wrinkled skin and my loose bladder! Not only did my skin become smooth but my cheeks regained their color!

Since then I haven't ever been sick as I take my vitamins regularly and eat right according to the health experts. I have my darling daughter to thank for this.

Through the years, while reading and keeping up with all the news on health, I found an article by Dr. Linus Pauling who received the Nobel Prize twice for his work on Vitamin C.

He suggested that at the first sign of a cold, you should take a 250 Vitamin C every hour. If you do this for 2 to 2 1/2 days, all the symptoms will disappear and then you gradually cut down every day to 2, 3, 4, and 5 hours or until you are taking you normal daily dose of 500 mg 3 times a day and you will never suffer from a cold.

It isn't the cold that's bad, it's the after affects which usually attack the weakest part of your body.

I have done this for many years and I haven't suffered from a cold since I started this treatment. Before, I used to have colds and bronchitis almost every few months.

Every body has a different sign that they are catching a cold and they should recognize it because the treatment is only effective if you take it in the beginning of a cold. My sign is that I ache in my shoulders. Some times, I mistake the ache in my shoulders for work I have done in the garden or other exercise. Twice in the last 30 years, I have mistaken the ache and, sure enough, I have had a cold.

CHAPTER THIRTY-EIGHT

UPON RECEIVING A PRIZE IN
A DRAMA FESTIVAL FOR A
PLAY I WROTE, ACTED IN AND
DIRECTED.

I also worked in a youth theater The director was an actress in one of the big theaters.

In one of the plays, I was coming down an inner hall with this gauzy dress and she had me do it over and over trying to force me to do it faster.

I explained to her that the material of the dress was catching on the rough walls but she didn't want to hear that and told me that I didn't know how to act in a theater.

My path is strewn with people who didn't like me for one reason or another but usually because they saw me as a threat.

There was a man who I had an affair with when my husband and I separated. At first, he was everything I wanted. He was connected with the theater and a wonderful lover.

After awhile, he began to show his true nature.

He began to complain about everything. The kind of complaints that have no logic and no end. If it was a rainy day, he wanted sunshine and if the sun was shining, it was too hot and sunny.

He ceased to be a wonderful lover and began to be very selfish and and thoughtless and demanding.

He kept pressing me to marry him but, by this time, I had no wish to do that. This made him furious and he wouldn't leave me alone.

My husband had just returned from America but I had no wish to be together with him again but I had to be with him to get rid of this man.

When the fellow saw that I really was again reunited with my husband, he left the country and he hasn't returned so I don't think there could be any danger from him, Ben. I'll give you his name if you wish.

==========

Today should be a good day. I was scheduled to have lunch with Sara.

Sara was such a nice person and had such a good sense of humor. Not having those qualities myself, I appreciated a sense of humor in others.

She lived so close to my apartment that I could walk and give my car a rest.

When I reached Sara's house, I could smell what she was cooking even out in the hall.

When she came to the door to let me in, I told her how good the meal smelled.

"Oh, that's not the meal," she said. "It's what I do to make people believe I'm a Cordon Bleu cook. I make a lot of compote and keep an onion roasting in my toaster oven."

I laughed. She was off again.

I noticed that her arm was bandaged and I asked what had happened.

She said that she had slipped and fallen and injured it on a flying trip to the ladies room in the theater.

"There's a message here but I haven't decoded it yet. I'm supposed to stay out of the theater or out of the ladies room. I don't know which yet"

And that's how the whole luncheon proceeded. I laughed more than I ate. It was a good meal, lots of salads that didn't have many calories.

After lunch, we settled down to talk.

"Have you made any progress on who could have done that to Ruth?" Sara wanted to know.

"I think I have. I think I know now why Ruth was killed, even though I'm not positive who could have done it."

"You mean you really know but you're not positive? Don't tell me! It's better I don't know so that even if they torture me, I won't be able to tell."

"Nobody's going to torture you, Sara. Where did you get that idea?"

"From the TV, where else? I seem to remember a movie with a plot like this."

"I'll tell you something shocking, though. I think that Ruth was blackmailing somebody and that's why she was killed!"

"No! That's hard to believe. I'm not being critical, judgmental or holier-than-thou. That would be arrogant as hell. Although I'm very brilliant and capable of straightening out the whole world, I don't have the answer to everything, yet, maybe next month."

Sara was so funny! But she could also be serious.

"I know she wanted an education in Drama very much."

"She talked of going to attend the Royal Academy in England. Yeah, lately she talked as though it was something in the near future. I thought she just fantasizing."

"That gives me an idea. I'll ask Mrs. Schwartz if Ruth received any mail from England or the United States. Maybe she wrote to places to register and I can find out something from that." I said.

"Good thinking. You know I'm a liberal. I think that everybody's entitled to my opinion."

Sara brought some coffee that she had been brewing and some small cookies.

'Those cookies look so innocent, don't they? Be warned. They're full of butter. If butter had legs, those cookies would be strolling all over this room and climbing up those draperies."

I noticed that Sara never laughed at her own jokes. She told them with a straight face and that made them funnier.

The cookies were delicious. I had one small one.

That's how I usually regulate my weight. I've convinced myself that if I take more than a taste of rich cakes and desserts, it will be just more of the same so why eat more.

It's just that sometimes 'more of the same' is exactly what I want.

CHAPTER THIRTY-NINE

The one bright spot in my life came from an unexpected source. A girlfriend of mine, whom I hadn't seen in ages, wrote a television series in English for teaching English in schools.

This was a bright amusing comedy and knowing me she wrote the part especially for me.

I was so appreciated by the director and the producer.

In one scene, I made a speech standing on a tractor about how the earth is our treasure and when I finished and walked by the producer, she said:

"And you are our treasure!"

I kept waiting for someone to foul up the works but it didn't happen and I had a ball. Also, since they kept on showing it twice a week, almost every day someone would recognize me from that program.

THE TELEVISION SERIES

Thinking about those times brought back memories that were pleasurable.

I got dressed, not too sexy an outfit because I wasn't that interested in Ben yet.

Dizengoff Street was where the cafe was situated that I was meeting Ben. It's the main street of Tel Aviv. It's lined with boutiques and restaurants and coffee houses.

The sidewalks are very wide so the cafe tables are usually outside.

In Tel Aviv, you can order a drink and sit with it for hours without getting dirty looks from the waiters.

As I walked along, I noticed some deterioration. It must be the influence of the Malls that are being built all over Israel.

Where, once, strolling down Dizengof Street was fun, now all the most prestigious places have moved to the malls.

The malls are also the place to take your children. The entertainment is free. That's one of the reasons I never go to them. The noise is repelling.

==========

My father had been very enthusiastic about the coffee houses of Israel.

"Frances, you don't have to sit in an office, You can conduct all your business sitting out in the fresh air or inside a coffee house. Everybody does it!"

He never made it to do business in a coffee house.

The rest of the family, especially my mother, never made a habit of sitting in a coffee house.

I don't like sitting in coffee houses myself. I just don't like gossiping or chatting, I guess.

I'm also very absent-minded. I should have been a professor.

Once, I parked my car downtown and when I came back to get it, it wasn't there.

So I took a bus to the place where they tow illegally parked cars but it wasn't there either.

I didn't know what to do. Had it been stolen?

I had some more things to do so I went back downtown to do them.

While walking down a street to reach a certain store, I spotted my car. I had forgotten where I had parked it and it was there, waiting for me on a different street. At home I took a short nap. I was meeting Ben that evening so I wanted to be rested so I'd have the patience to deal with him. Fifteen minutes is all I need to cut the day in two. I wake up feeling refreshed and with new energy.

CHAPTER FORTY

Ben was already sitting at a table and waiting for me. I wasn't hungry so I ordered just a cup of tea.

"Did you find out anything from Ralph?" He went straight to the point.

"How did you know I saw Ralph? You said that you weren't following me yesterday evening."

"I saw him today," Ben said. "And he told me. Why, was it supposed to be a secret?"

I hoped I wasn't blushing.

"No, of course not." I told Ben and then I choked on my tea.

Only I can choke on a cup of tea!. It seems that my vocal chords don't come together the way they should.

I once had precancerous polyps on my vocal chords but I cleared them without an operation.

The doctor, the theater sent me to, warned me not to let them operate on my vocal chords.

He looked at my throat and told me that I would never be able to become an actress. Just one more in a line of people who didn't think I could make it.

He said I didn't talk in my natural register and I would have to pitch my speaking tone much higher. There he was right.

He had me hold my hands over my face and hum. Where my humming was the strongest, was where my voice should have been pitched. Under the influence of Hollywood movies, I had been talking in a too low voice.

In my next visit to that doctor I talked in a higher voice and he was amazed. He told me that it usually took a long time for a person to change their register.

Screaming would clear the polyps he told me.

Well I screamed enough in 'Who's Afraid of Virginia Woolf' to take care of that.

That doctor was so right. Julie Andrews had her polyps removed surgically and she can't sing anymore.

The outcome with me was that my vocal chords didn't meet and it is very easy for me to choke on anything.

Also, I was left with a hoarse tone to my voice. Which is not unpleasant. I've noticed that most actresses have it too.

The only trouble is that when I choke, at first I sound like I'm going to die.

WHO'S AFRAID OF VIRGINIA WOLF F

Ben knew the Heimlich method of saving a person from choking to death. He came in back of me and put his arms around me and squeezed. I tried to tell him that I didn't need it but I couldn't get a word out. Besides he was enjoying squeezing me so much.

Finally, I stopped choking and could explain the whole story to him. He went back to his seat and smiled, so self satisfied.

'I felt so good hugging you. I could do with more of that."

"Ben, "I explained to him, "in the Heimlich maneuver you're supposed to hug a person around his diaphragm, not his breast."

"I know," he answered, "but it's more fun my way."

What could I say? He was right.

I gave him all the sheets that I had typed and he looked them over while I finished drinking my tea.

"This isn't much," he said after reading what I had given him.

"Well, it's the story of my sad life up to a certain point. Of didn't you notice how sad it was?"

"Yes, I noticed but it doesn't help me in my investigation."

"I told you it wouldn't, didn't I?"

"I'm sure that you left out some important parts, probably because you wanted to forget them. The psychiatrists say that we bury that kind of information in order to protect ourselves but it harms us to hide it and their job is to reveal that information to ourselves.

"So what do you suggest? That I go to a psychiatrist?"

"That wouldn't be such a bad idea."

"And who's going to pay for it? You know how much they cost, don't you?"

"Just one visit will probably do it. You aren't neurotic or anything like that, are you? You can afford one visit, can't you?"

"Why should I?"

"It might do you some good, too. I think all actors are neurotic, otherwise they wouldn't be actors.

"You sound like you don't like the theater."

"I'll tell you my reaction to the various snippets of scenes from 'plays and musicals categories. The dialogue seems forced and unnatural and the situations bizarre. The music, much of it , sounds dissonant, almost unsingable and thoroughly non-melodic. Someone, I can't remember who, said that when the arts become bizarre, it's a sign that civilization is going down the tube. And this is one of my more cheerful days."

"I don't believe in psychiatrists." I stated

"So what do you suggest?" he asked?

"I'll go home and try to think of anything I might have left out or forgotten to write about."

"Are you sure you don't want me to come home with you and ask you questions that might remind you of things you have forgotten and haven't written about?"

"I told you, my house is a mess. I've taken all the things that got soaked on the roof inside to dry and not only is the house upside down, it smells of wet wool."

"You don't write much about your first husband. Are you in touch with him?"

"Not willingly."

"Then how do you know that he doesn't harbor bad feelings towards you?"

"He hates this country and wouldn't come here if you paid him. Anyway, I've heard that he remarried and has a daughter who is as fat as a house and I'm sure that happened in reaction to his behavior to her. He's also got a mother-in-law living with him who is over a hundred years old. I figure he's got enough on his plate without worrying about me."

"You seem to know a lot about him."

"He writes to the children a few times a year and I have friends in the town in Michigan where he lives."

"So why didn't you include all this information?"

"I figured it wasn't relevant."

"Well, stop trying to figure out what's relevant or not relevant and write down everything." He was almost shouting, he was so angry.

I didn't have to be a psychiatrist to know that he wasn't angry about what I was leaving out. He was angry at my not responding to his overtures.

I didn't know what to do about it so I just pretended that he was angry at me.

I just gave a meek nod, said 'thank you for the tea' and left him sitting there, too surprised to react quickly enough.

CHAPTER FORTY-ONE

The next morning, my sleep was interrupted very early.

A man I didn't know was at the door.

I saw him through the small window and asked him what he wanted.

He told me that he had come to see if there was any mail for him. I was shocked!

I opened the door and let him enter.

"Did you live here before me?" I asked him.

"Yes, of course. Otherwise how could mail have come for me?"

He looked at me as if I were some king of idiot. There was, however, a method to my madness.

"Why did you move, may I ask?"

"You may. The police sent me a notice that this place had been built illegally and so I had to leave. Have they now issued a permit for the apartment?

"No, I got the same notice. What happened to the money that you paid for the apartment?"

"The contractor reimbursed me."

"How did you get him to do that?"

"I told him I'd break his bones if he didn't give me back my money. Why all these questions? Wait a minute, were you stuck the same way?"

"Yes!"

"Wow!"

I started to dance around him.

"If you weren't such a stranger, I'd kiss you"

I could see him edging towards the door and looking at me strangely.

"No, please. I'm not crazy. You just saved my life, or a least all my money. Maybe that amounts to the same thing. What a fortuitous series of circumstances!"

"I'm sorry, I don't understand." The poor guy was so confused. He didn't know what to make of me.

"Let me explain. I bought this apartment in good faith. After I got the same notice you did from the police I asked the contractor to give me back my money. He refused But now," I just couldn't stop laughing. "but now, don't you see? I can threaten to go to the police and tell them that he sold me the apartment when he knew already that it was illegal and he'll have to reimburse me or go to jail."

I couldn't stop laughing .

"Now, oh joy, I'm going to make him pay for all the damages and my moving expenses. Yippie! I'm saved. About your mail, if there is any I'll send it to you. Just write your name and address here"

He gave me his business card. His name was Jack Barman and he was an insurance salesman.

"Would you like a drink? Can I give you anything to eat? Here's some chocolate. Do me a favor and eat it, I'm supposed to be on a diet"

I laid out the chocolate and some cheese crackers and put on the kettle.

He thanked me but he said he didn't have time to stay. He said he was very happy for me and would do anything he could to help.

What a nice person. I wish he had stayed.

After he left, I took off my shoes and danced around the room. I didn't want to antagonize the neighbors living below me. I might need them.

Then I sat down at my computer and added this story to what I was going to hand to Ben.

Now that I was up already and in a good mood I was ready to add more to my life story and try to finish it.

CHAPTER FORTY-TWO

About this time, I heard that the National Theater wanted to find an actress to replace someone in the play, 'Who's Afraid of Virginia Woolf?'. The original actress was pregnant and couldn't go on.

I tried out for it and got the part. The dialogue called for me to swear. In English, it's hard for me to swear. I wasn't brought up that way. In Hebrew where I barely understood what I was saying, it was a piece of cake.

This leads to another saga which is not so fascinating as it is aggravating so I'll just give you the essentials.

When I agreed to do the part, they promised me that they would bring the critics to see it again. It was a 3 ½ hour production full of monologues for me.

When the actress whose place I was taking saw how well I did it, she refused to let the critics see it.

She had more clout there than I did.

Our theaters in Israel are socialistic. When the actor, after four years, receives tenure they can't be fired except for moral or criminal charges. Not for refusing to do a part or for lousy acting.

One of the actresses in this theater is so bad that she hasn't been given a part for years but they can't fire her and she still receives her salary!

When I came here from Michigan, so many years ago and wanted to become an actress on the Israeli stage, they said: "Forget it!".

No Anglo-Saxon adult had succeeded in losing their accent sufficiently to be accepted for the Hebrew Theater.

An Anglo-Saxon is anyone coming from a country where they speak English.

Telling me that I am unable to do something is like waving a red flag in front of a bull....me being the bull. I love a challenge. I did it but it took me a long time.

I left another production to do this one but I had a great deal of difficulty concentrating on the 3 1/2 hours of text and I couldn't sleep at night.

I had this terrible feeling that I wasn't going to make it.

Then I remembered that in the production that I had left, one of the fellows had once hypnotized us after a show when we were stuck in the little town of Safad with nothing to do.

I remembered that he had particularly been successful with me.

I got in touch with him, told him my problem and asked him if he could possibly help me.

I was overjoyed when he said: "Sure!" And help me he did!.

In Safad, I remember that after he put me in the hypnotic trance, he told me to go back to the days when I first came to Israel, when I was in the communal settlement up north - Kfar Giladi.

I had removed my shoes as I was telling about my life there and as I rubbed my feet over the tiled floor, I said:

"Oh, I must be careful or I'll tear my stockings on this wooden floor."

I really thought that I was back in the wooden floored cabin in the commune although the floor beneath my feet now was a smooth tile floor.

Then he told me that five minutes after I awakened, I would see a funny movie on the opposite wall.

He snapped me our of my trance and I laughed and said:

"I remember what you told me. I wasn't under that deep. I'm sure I won't see any funny movie."

That's what I thought. I saw the funny movie and laughed my head off. It appears that I am a very easy person to hypnotize.

I think I knew that and the only reason I had let this man hypnotize me was that I trusted him completely. I had refused other offers to hypnotize me before this.

We made a date and sat in my car as he first asked me what I wanted to accomplish. I wanted to implant in my subconscious that I could easily learn the part and I could sleep at night.

He hypnotized me, gave me those commands and from then on, I was able to learn my part and sleep well at night.

This actor friend was such a caring person that he came to my theater before my first performance and hypnotized me while I was on the stage waiting for the curtain to lift and told me that I wouldn't make any mistakes, and I didn't.

For some reason, he never wanted to help me again and I really needed his help.

I can only think that they wanted me to fail when they gave me another leading part in the play 'Misunderstanding' by Camus. I played the daughter and the first lady of the theater played my mother.

It was difficult doing both parts and I believe that they gave me the second part hoping that I would fail.

Lady Peggy Ashcroft was in the audience that evening and she wrote in an article that I and the actress who was the most lauded in Israel and played my mother were both great.

After that they never let me see another director. I was given smaller parts. The next play had me doing two small parts and although I had a minor role in both, the stagehands told me in the dress rehearsal that I was stealing the show. The stagehands always know better than anyone else what's happening in a show.

This actor had one of the leading parts and was furious that I was getting so much attention. Before we could open with the show, he succeeded in convincing the management that this was a Nazi play and they removed it.

This same actor was the one who had informed on me to Sophia Loren and ruined my part in both plays because, as the saying goes, I was stealing the show.

Never mind that it was an expensive production and they were losing a lot of money by canceling it.

My wonderful luck, every time I did something well something or someone would ruin it for me.

CHAPTER FORTY-THREE

The next morning I had a whole day with nothing to do. I looked at my diary to make sure.

Next week I had to go to court and testify against my contractor.

It seems that somebody else had put in a complaint about him.

I knew that I would have to start looking for another apartment but I didn't feel like doing that. I felt like leaving the country for awhile.

Maybe I would go back to the USA to get my High School diploma. But I didn't want to leave until I had solved the problem of who had murdered Ruth.

What I wanted to do next was meet with Dora, the widow of Sam, the actor who had made so much trouble for me.

Could he have hated me so much that he tried to murder me?

Sure, I fit into the category of people who threatened his career.

I couldn't believe that someone would use that as an excuse to commit murder.

The man had died of a heart attack about a week after Ruth had died. So who was doing all these things against me?

Could it be that he wasn't alone and his friends were involved?

Maybe he had said something to his wife before he died. I kind of hoped he was the villain. I know he was in the theater when it happened.

I called his wife and she said she didn't have any free time until the day after tomorrow so we settled on that day at 4:00.

I had some free time and didn't feel like writing about my life any more so I called Sara and asked her if she felt like having another go at the cafe in the theater.

She said sure and we made a date for 2:00. That would be when all the actors were finishing their rehearsals and most of them would come to the cafe.

Sara was already sitting a a table and waiting for me. We both had a salad and then Sara ordered apple pie and ice cream.

She saw me looking at her and said:

"I'm hungry, damn it! A year ago, I lost 22 pounds, from my face. I got up in the middle of the night to go to the bathroom and looked in the mirror. I almost had a hemorrhage. I thought it was Frankenstein."

"I still think you would make a lovely actress even as plump as you are," I told her. "Or you could even have liposuction. It isn't dangerous at all. At the seminar I went to last month on plastic surgery, the doctor even tells his patients to gain weight so that he can drain more fat out of them."

"How could I? Have you forgotten my blocked brain? I tried to take a course in literature a few months ago...no way. Learning is now a battle of wits between me and my brain cells. I put the information in, it tosses it right out again. I put it back in, my brain tosses it out again. If I keep at it long enough and repeat the procedure at intervals thereafter, the brain boss grudgingly lets it in...one tiny piece at a time and on a trial basis!"

I laughed. Sara was so good comical about her faults.

"But tell me the name of that doctor. I'd like to get fatter so that I can get thinner. I like that idea a lot."

"I'll have to look it up when I get home. I'll call you."

"But what would the doctor do with all the extra skin I would have sagging there.?"

"Well, he said that usually the skin shrinks back. He doesn't like to operate and do a tummy tuck. He said that those are really dangerous.

"An honest doctor. I like him. I have a girlfriend who had plastic surgery on her nose and she had a small cancerous spot removed. Now her nostrils don't match and it looks like she just smelled something foul. The doctor assured her that it should go back to it's original shape. If it doesn't, that doctor better be a fast runner."

Just then a cockroach crawled under our table. Well, this is a tropical country and cockroaches are part of it.

When Sara saw it, she laughed and said that she had heard of a sure way to kill cockroaches. Cockroaches can be killed by putting out a cheap bowl of wine. They drink the wine, get tipsy and fall in and drown. With slugs, you use beer. They are a lower class bug."

And that's the way our lunch went, full of laughs. None of the actors came up to us. Most of them just nodded hello and some didn't even do that. Maybe they were afraid that if they became friendly with me, they would be killed as Ruth was.

I was fantasizing with Sara about what I would choose if a genie offered me just one wish. My former youth or my former good hearing. (I was having some trouble with it.)

There was no genie around but I wavered between what most people would consider vital and frivolous. I think it's an interesting commentary that I hesitated as I did. We're getting these messages from our environment or from the media. There's racism, sexism and agism and they're all reinforced by the media."

Sara's comment was:

"Maybe you are of the opinion that anything that is expensive should at least be chocolate and edible? Absolutely right!"

That lunch really cheered me up.

It was already 4:00 and I was getting sleepy so I walked Sara home. I had a nap and then I wrote some more of my rotten luck.

========

Feeling frustrated after leaving the Haifa Theater, I talked the stage manager there into coming to Tel Aviv and directing me in a commercial production - 'The Trial of Mary Dugan.

I introduced him to some of the actors I knew in Tel Aviv in order to help him maybe obtain a job.

He did better. He fired me from the cast and took the wife of an important member of a theater, gave her the part and made a deal with that actor to direct a play at his theater next season. Of course it was the same actor, Sam!

In firing me, I got into an argument with the producer of the production, Menahem Golan.

This producer made many films and became an important person in the film industry in Hollywood and then in Israel.

The result was that he wouldn't let me play in any one of his movies for 20 years.

He actually cut me out of a few films I had been chosen to do.

After that I suppose he forgot. I made two movies for him. 'Thunder Warriors'

(Now called 'America, 3000') and 'Delta Force'.

I suppose I should be grateful that I have succeeded in working in the theater and films and TV when so many actors are praying for a chance to act but why did so many bad things have to happen to me?

Every time it looked as if I would be a great success something happened to trip me up.

I warned you, Ben. You know, don't you, you're getting a stream of consciousness talk here. It's boring and I apologize. I plead brain rot. Tomorrow I'll try to make it more interesting. Maybe I'll lie a little.

CHAPTER FORTY-FOUR

The next morning I finally had the time to call my lawyer and tell him what I had learned about my apartment. He said he would take care of calling the contractor and getting my money back for me. He said that he wouldn't charge me for that because it was the least he could do for me.

I wanted to finish this dreary task so I sat down determined to end it.

First, I'll catch up on my family life.

==========

My two boys went to an agriculture boarding school. This was the only solution to their problem.

I didn't want them stuck helping my husband on the farm and not be able to graduate High School.

After we left the farm, my older son Hal couldn't make it even in the boarding school so he left to be a cowboy on a Commune. He told me that he rode a horse and carried an Uzi machine gun while he watched over a small herd of cattle.

I knew he was trying to scare me so I kept my cool and told him to be sure to keep the gun pointed away from his feet.

After awhile, I decided to send him to his father in America because I knew he'd never get anywhere without a High School diploma. The level of education was much lower in the States and also, since English was his mother tongue, it would be easier for him.

I had forgotten how dictatorial and cruel, my first husband had been.

At graduation time, Hal thought he wasn't going to graduate and was afraid of his father. I had forgotten the way his father had treated him. When he was very young, his father had shouted at him when he made a slight noise with the cutlery while he was eating. As a result, Hal's throat closed up and he couldn't swallow anything that wasn't ground up. He also talked slightly through his nose.

He begged me to send him a ticket to come back to Israel before the graduation.

Not only didn't I have enough money but I thought it would be bad for him to run away from his problems.

The outcome was that he ran away and enlisted in the Navy, like his half brother.

My first husband had remarried and her son was in the Navy.

Although it turned out that he had succeeded in graduating, the Navy was good for him because he needed a strong framework to take the place of his father. Hal, however, to this day holds it against me that I didn't want him to come home. I certainly didn't want him to come back to taking care of cattle.

The younger boy, Marshall couldn't join his brother at the agriculture boarding school for quite a long time. The trouble was that even at the age of 13 he still wet his bed. This was because his father, when he was two years old would grab the sleeping child and throw him out of bed when he saw that it was wet. Marshall badly wanted to join his brother at the school but they wouldn't accept a bed-wetter. We tried every thing even electric shock but nothing helped. Finally, the next year, the wish to join his brother miraculously stopped his wetting.

I think this helps to explain some of the reasons why I so desperately wanted to leave my first husband and why I was so happy when he left.

My daughter was too young when he left to be influenced by him.

At an early age, she wanted to learn ballet and, although I took her to ballet class in Israel for a few years, the best place was in England. At the age of nine, I took her to Tunbridge Wells in Kent, England, to a Russian school highly recommended by her ballet teacher.

It wasn't only for the dancing. She was a very poor sport and would never admit that she had lost at a game. Also she was very clumsy and walked and talked like a boy. She was imitating her brothers.

When we arrived at the school in England, the headmistress looked her over and then told her she could go and take a bath.

"I no want bath!" She shocked the headmistress by talking back to her.

When it came time to say goodbye, the tears were rolling down my cheeks but my stalwart daughter only said:

"Goodbye, mudder, you can go now!"

Thank goodness she had never been afraid of anything as a child.

When she came to join us, my second husband and I, in New York the first summer, she had a lovely Queen's English accent and we loved to hear her talk. She also had lovely manners, a well modulated voice and had grown quite a bit. As a friend of mine remarked:

"Anna, your hands no longer reach your knees!"

Anna came flying home the next summers with a tag on her blouse and the school would send me a telegram so that I could meet her at the airport.

One summer the telegram didn't arrive. I was performing and couldn't be reached. Luckily, a friend of my older son was working at the airport and gave Anna the money for a taxi. I came home and found my little girl asleep on my doorstep.

I never got any of the money my father left when he died so my brother, who took all the money, paid for the boarding school for the boys and all expenses for Anna. I could have used that money but I was glad to use it on the children.

One of the reasons that I wanted the children in boarding schools was my second husband's attitude to them. He couldn't bond with my older son, Hal and he couldn't stand my daughter. The only one he would pay any attention to was my younger son. The other children felt it and it saddened and frustrated them.

Also, my mother spoiled them and bribed them with gifts of money and kept talking to them about how terrible it was that their mother was an actress.

When she retired, at the age of 75, I was supposed to run the tile factory that she had been running.

I was busy in the theater so I let my son and my husband run it.

It was their bad luck that there was a recession that year and they had to close the place. They paid all the workers and their debts with the money I got when I sold my beautiful apartment on the hill overlooking the Mediterranean.

CHAPTER FORTY-FIVE

I came home, ate, had a short nap and then I went to the market to buy the roast chicken and wine for my dinner with Ralph. I shiver when I remember what happened to me the last time I went to a market. Perhaps I should say what nearly happened to me.

==========

That had been in the famous Mahane Yehuda market in Jerusalem.

I went to buy some things, mostly thread and some mascara from a little shop on the open side of the market. It was quite inexpensive there compared with the larger shops in town.

The roofed side of the market was on the other side of the wall and there they sold a great selection of only meats, fish, fruits and vegetables.

I loved shopping there but that day I was too tired or in a hurry to get home, I don't remember which but certainly my personal little angel was watching over me.

In the little shop, suddenly the whole place shook.

I thought at first it was an earthquake. It reminded me of Nicaragua

We all rushed outside and that's when we saw the people, all bloody and panicky running out of the roofed section of the market.

Two suicide bombers had exploded themselves there.

I didn't stay there. I couldn't. I took a taxi home and sat there shaking for a long time.

After that they closed the entrances and exits and placed soldiers there to examine anyone coming in.

==========

I went to the Tel Aviv downtown market. It was not far from the seashore of the lovely Mediterranean and I loved walking along the boardwalk since it had been redecorated with colorful tiles and seats.

This market was very open and wouldn't do as much damage if a suicide bomber blew himself up here.

I feel so sorry for the poor young Arab boys. They are told that they would go to heaven and to Paradise with lovely young virgins to keep them company.

I bought my roast chicken and the wine and took a taxi home.

I was too upset to write more after remembering my almost demise so I didn't go back to the computer to write more.

I took a book to read, had supper , read some more and slept.

CHAPTER FORTY-SIX

I woke up the next morning and began to sing while I took my shower. I hadn't done that for a long time.

I can't really sing well although I have sung leading roles on stage. Mostly, I holler good.

Both my husbands were good singers and they couldn't stand my singing so I had to stop that cheerful little habit.

I must have been really looking forward to the meal with Ralph.

I couldn't decide what to wear.

It was a shame my blue trouser suit was ruined. It would have been perfect.

I didn't even want to look at it, it reminded me of Ruth and what had happened to her.

I found an older brown suit that wasn't too bad and I put it on with some flashy earrings.

I took the chicken and the wine and got in my car. It was easier to find the way in the daytime.

Ralph was waiting for me and answered the door on my first ring. He took the packages, put the chicken to warm in the oven and the wine in the refrigerator.

Then we sat in the living room and talked. It was so easy to talk to Ralph. He complimented me on what I was wearing and said that he had also liked the blue suit with the embroidery that I wore.

That stopped me cold!

I had only worn that suit on the day of the murder. I didn't have time to concentrate on when he could have seen me wearing the blue suit. I filed that away in my mind for future contemplation.

Ralph must have seen my puzzled look but he didn't comment on it.

After we finished eating and I went to the door to say goodbye, Ralph insisted on taking me to my car.

He didn't try to get too familiar. He just hugged me lightly and kissed my cheek. I liked that he didn't try to get more intimate even though he must have noticed me blushing and how I reacted to him.

"I want to see you again." he said. "I'll call you and we'll meet again, okay?"

"Of course." I answered and sat in the driver's seat. I waved goodbye and rode off.

We had talked so long and I hadn't noticed that it was already twilight.

While I was still driving in Jaffa, I noticed a car coming up close to me. It came around and bumped my side. At first I thought it was a mistake and I moved away but it moved and bumped me harder.

I looked around and saw that I was on the edge of a ravine where they were excavating a building and if he didn't stop bumping me I could go over. The place was fenced in but I could crash right through the wooden fence.

What was this? Was it an attempt to kill me or just to put me in the hospital for awhile? Was Ben right? Had that bar that came crashing down really had been meant to kill me? I looked around desperately but the street was deserted.

I really felt I was in danger so I tried an unexpected move. I backed up and quickly made a U turn and drove back until I saw a cafe. I parked and ran in and called Ben on his cell phone. Luckily I got him.

"Ben, I'm in danger, someone is trying to kill me!"

"Where are you?"

I didn't know so I asked the waiter the address. I gave it to Ben and he said:

"Stay there. I'll send a policeman there who is on duty near you and I'll be there as soon as I can.

I sat down and ordered some coffee and a piece of cake that I couldn't eat but I wanted the waiter near me. I asked him when he came over:

"What kind of place is this?"

"It's a cafe." he said looking at me queerly.

"Do you serve meals?" I wanted to keep him near me.

"Sure!"

"What kind?"

By that time, the policeman came in, thank goodness.

"Please sit beside me," I told him. And please have this cake. I'm too nervous to eat it."

"It's alright," I told the surprised waiter. "I called the police because someone tried to kill me."

I told the policeman that I was waiting for Ben the detective. I couldn't even remember his last name I was so nervous and frightened.

I had to tell the policeman the entire story. I don't know if he believed me but when Ben arrived, I saw the policeman was a bit more convinced that I wasn't just a hysterical female.

"Ben!" I cried out when I saw him entering. "Oh, am I glad to see you." I hugged him him when he came closer.

"So do you still think that bar wasn't meant to kill you?"

"I don't know what to think, Ben. Maybe all this is happening because I'm getting too close to finding out who killed her and why?

"Boy! You are one stubborn woman. I think I'll have a cup of coffee while I'm here. I rushed so fast to get here.

"I can't thank you enough, Ben."

Ben asked the waiter for some coffee and then started to interrogate me. What are you doing in Jaffa, Fran?"

"I thought you were still following me and knew everywhere I went and what I was doing."

"I know you went to visit Ralph but that was hours ago."

"Oh, we sat and talked a long time, I guess."

Ben peered at me closely but I wasn't blushing so he relaxed and drank his coffee.

"I guess I'm going to have to put a man on surveillance on you."

"That would be nice but can you spare someone to do that?"

"Well, since your apartment is so messed up, you could come and stay with me."

"No, that would be too much. I have to work and I need my things," I tried to let Ben down without insulting him.

"Okay, I'll put on a man to watch over you until I can finish with this. I think I'm close to discovering who's behind it."

We left the cafe with Ben following me home.

When we reached my apartment, he got out of the car and came over to me.

"I've called for a man to sit in a car in front of your apartment. Here's his cell phone number. His name is David." Ben handed me his card with a number written on the front and another on the back.

The number on the front is my private home number and the one in back is my cell phone number."

Ben took me up to my apartment, looked around in the bathroom and the closet and the roof.

"Take care of yourself," he said, then he kissed my cheek and left.

I was too nervous to rest or read so I tried to finish up my life story.

CHAPTER FORTY-SEVEN

Around this time I was called to come to Jerusalem to direct a play in English for a theater that was just starting up.

The people didn't tell me that they had already put on one performance and it was a failure.

So I went ahead, rented an apartment in Jerusalem and put on the play. 'Separate Tables'.

It was a great success.

I wasn't happy, however doing just English theater in Israel. I felt that we could do original Hebrew plays in English. I was good enough now in Hebrew so that I could translate the plays from Hebrew into English.

I was busy directing my second play when the man who founded the theater and brought me to direct came and started to complain that I was taking too much time and he needed the next performance in 2 weeks.

I couldn't do that and have a good performance so I told him that it was impossible.

The man then said that I was acting too bossy and he was thinking of firing me.

So I quit!

That's when I decided to start my own theater and compete with him.

Things went very well at first. I had good audiences and write ups in the newspapers. I also made a little money. Not much at first but at least I wasn't losing money at first.

I translated several Israeli play into English and put them on.

I did a lot of the work myself. I made the posters, the costumes, the scenery and the props. I also directed and did the lighting for the show and kept the books.

I even wrote one of the plays and directed and acted in it and we received first prize when I entered it in that year's Drama Festival.

Then I lost my audiences. It was a great disappointment to me when I found that the English speaking public in Israel was more interested in nostalgic large cast musicals that the other group was putting on

Having a large cast brought all their friends and relatives to see them even though the shows were badly done.

The last show I did was an artistic success.

My girlfriend wrote a biblical play and I made it into a very successful musical.

The play was about Abraham, Sarah and Hagar and called 'The Eternal Triangle' It was also a comedy with 3 dancing girls – (The servants in the house)

We could have had a long run but the girls had to leave for some reason and I couldn't find replacements.

By that time, I was very tired doing everything by myself and I closed the theater.

I had no one to help me, The fellow I was working with wanted me to have an affair with him and I didn't care enough about him to do that.

Oh, well such is life!

CHAPTER FORTY-EIGHT

The next morning I slept badly, I finally took a sleeping pill at 2:00 and didn't wake up until nine. It was good that my meeting with Dora, wasn't until the afternoon.

I was glad that Ben hadn't called me early in the morning as he usually did.

Just then the phone rang and it was Ben.

"Hi Fran, how are you feeling?"

"Not too good, Ben, I had to take a sleeping pill to sleep last night."

"Good you had one handy.'

"I just love how you sympathize with me! Listen, I'm going to a meeting with Dora, Sam's, wife, this afternoon and maybe I can find out what's going on."

"Where's the meeting?"

"In the Habima Theater Cafe."

"Lots of people and waiters there?"

"Sure!"

"Don't go anywhere else with her and watch what you're eating and drinking.

"Why? Is she connected with anything that happened?"

"No, but her husband was."

"But he's not living anymore, is he?"

"No, but be careful."

"Gosh, you're scaring me. I think I'll ask that guy you've got watching me to come in and sit near us in case anything happens."

"Good idea, Fran, I'll call you tonight, bye.

"I drank some coffee for breakfast but I couldn't eat anything after that conversation with Ben . He didn't mention my life story so maybe he doesn't need it anymore, I hope!"

I went out on the roof and rested in the sun until noon.

Sitting there, I remembered what Ralph had said about my blue suit and I realized that he couldn't have seen me in it unless he had been in the theater the day that Ruth was murdered!

That was an awesome thought.

But he had said that he wasn't there that day! Was he involved with the near accident when I left his house?

Was that why he went to call someone right after he mentioned the blue suit?

I should have mentioned it to Ben.

I went inside my room and dialed Ben's number but all I got was a message to leave a message.

I hoped that Ralph wasn't involved. ate a sandwich with cheese and lettuce and another cup of decaf coffee and then I went back to bed for a nap. I was completely out mentally and physically.

As tired as I was I called Sara, but only her voice mail answered and I left a message hoping she was well and that I'd call again in the morning.

I called David, the surveillance man and asked him to come to the Habima Theater Cafe across the street and sit near me but not to act as if he knew me.

It was so convenient to just walk across the street to get to the theater. I sure hoped I could keep the apartment.

Dora was sitting next to the wall and waiting for me when I entered. I wondered if she still resented me because she had failed so miserably in that part she took away from me. She gave me a faint smile as I sat across from her. I ordered a bottle of lemonade and asked for a straw not a glass. David came in and sat not far away.

"Well, Fran, what can you possibly want to talk to me about?"

"It's about your late husband, Sam..."

"Why can't you just leave him alone? He's not living anymore so there's really nothing to talk about is there?"

Not only her words but her tone was so belligerent that I was stunned and didn't know how to continue.

"Well, I just wanted to know if he ever said anything to you about Ruth. Had she ever tried to blackmail him?" I blurted out.

There it was out. I didn't beat around the bush, I just said it.

"Why you rotten little bitch! What would she have to blackmail him about? He wasn't involved with what was going on in the theater! How could you think such a thing?"

Her voice was getting louder and people turned around to look at us so I didn't answer her for a few moments.

"Dora, you know that Ruth was murdered. That was no accident. They found that the rope had been cut. And maybe it was meant for me. The brake fluid container in my car was punctured and I almost had an accident and someone tried yesterday to push me into a ravine. I'm frightened and I'm trying to find out who's doing it. It couldn't have been Sam because he isn't around anymore but maybe he told you something about what's going on here."

"No, he only said once that some people here are making a lot of money from the redecorating, but that's all he said about it."

"Thank you, Dora, I'll tell that to Ben, the detective in charge. Maybe that will help him solve the case. He's got me writing my whole life story trying to find who hates me enough to want to kill me." I gave a short mocking laugh.

"Thanks for meeting with me, Dora, I hope this didn't upset you too much."

"No," she said. "I hope it helps."

I hoped so too and I couldn't wait to tell Ben what she had said.

I paid the bill, nodded to a few people I knew and went back to my apartment.

CHAPTER FORTY-NINE

As I walked into my one room apartment, I could see the telephone flashing that I had a message. I thought it was probably Ben impatient to find out what I had learned from Dora.

It wasn't. It was a call from a hospital telling me that Sara wanted to talk to me.

My heart was pounding as I waited to hear her voice.

"Sara, is that you? Are you alright? What happened?"

"Oh, Fran, I'm alright now but it was so painful."

"What happened to you?"

Sara was crying so hard I could hardly make out what she said.

"They broke my fingers! I was seized in my apartment. When I woke up I was in another place and four men in ski masks so I couldn't see who they were, had me tied in a chair and were shouting at me. They wanted to know if Ruth had ever talked to me and what she had said. You remember I told you once that I didn't want to know what was going on so that nobody could torture me and find out what I knew and you said that only happened on TV". Sara was sobbing as she talked to me. "I was so glad I didn't know anything. I think they

191

would have killed me if I had known something. Something scared them and they untied me and ran away. I found a taxi and came to the hospital. I didn't call the police because they warned me that If I called the police they would kill me.'

"Sara, I'm coming right over! Hold tight until I get there!"

'No, no," she screamed. "Stay away from me...for your sake and for mine!"

"Alright, Sara, don't cry."

"They called a taxi to take me home."

Maybe it was foolish but I just couldn't leave Sara there alone in her apartment and crying. The man sitting outside my apartment would follow me and take care of me if anything happened.

So I waited an hour and then walked over to Sara's place.

David had followed me and I told him that if I didn't come out in 15 minutes, he should call Ben.

I went in and knocked on Sara's door.

Two men, wearing ski masks and long robes, stood in the open door and grabbed me and held me while another man, also dressed the same way, bound my hands in back of me, sat me in a chair and tied my feet.

Sara was sitting tied in a chair with a piece of tape over her mouth.

Her eyes held a look of terror and the tears streamed down her face.

"What do you know about Ruth," They asked me. The man whispered so I couldn't tell who he was.

I tried to play dumb but they didn't accept that. I'm an actress but I was so frightened that I couldn't play the part.

Then they took a pair of pliers and began to pull at my fingernails. That was horribly painful and I screamed.

"Wait, I'll tell you what I know!"

"Sara groaned and one of the men slapped her face hard.

"Don't hurt her. She doesn't know anything. I'll tell you what I know although it isn't much. Ruth wanted to be an actress and she wanted to go to England and study there but she didn't have enough money so I think she tried blackmail. I don't know what she was blackmailing about and who she was blackmailing and that's all I know."

"You do know what Ruth knew and what she was blackmailing about and who she was blackmailing and you're going to tell us everything you know."

I knew the best think was to spin some kind of tale and gain some time so that David who was guarding me could get help and come and rescue us.

It had probably something to do with the redecorating the theater was undergoing but I have no idea exactly what or who it could have been

"We think a little pain will help you think better."

So they started in on my nails again all I could do was scream.

They put another piece of tape over my mouth. I don't know how long I could hold out.

Just then, the door burst open and a whole bunch of policemen came running in and took the men into custody.

They untied me and Sara fainted. I and some of the men put her on the sofa and covered her.

Ben gave me a disgusted look.

`But when he saw how pitiful I looked, he put his arms around me.

"Don't worry, Fran. We'll put those men in jail. They're actors and workers in the theater. They were embezzling some of the money that was given for redecorating the theater. Ruth was blackmailing them and so they killed her. One of them was driving the truck that tried to bump you into the ravine. Your friend Ralph was also involved. He's the one who called the man in the truck. I don't know why they went after you but maybe you'll be able to clear that up.

"I know why, Ben. Ralph made a bad mistake when he told me that he had liked me in my blue suit with the embroidered pocket. The first time I wore that suit was the afternoon of the murder and it was so splattered with Ruth's blood that I couldn't wear it again. Ralph told the police and also told me that he wasn't there that day.

"So," Ben said. "It was really Ruth they meant to kill and not you at first.'

`'Yes, I was right about that and you didn't want to listen to me. I had to write about my whole rotten life."

"I'm glad you did, Fran. I wonder if you would have told me all of it without that as an excuse. You know I'm interested in you and want to know all about you.

I liked Ben better now, but only as a friend. I don't think it will go any farther. Who knows?"

About my apartment. I lost it and had to move. When I went back to see it a year later, I found that a Police Sergeant was living in it.

THE END

194

The story of the murder is a fictionized tale.

Except for the end. Some people were jailed for embezzling money in the Habima Theater during the redecorations.

The story of my life is true.

And also that end it true, When I went back to my apartment, I saw the mailbox and the name of a police Sergeant was written there.

Films

WILLIAM KENNEDY AND I IN - 'DELTA FORCE'

THE FILM – AMERICA 30000

Plays That I Performed In

A FRENCH FARCE

A HEBREW PLAY

NO EXIT

'TA RA RA BOOMTIAY'

'THE BOY FRIEND'

'THE FOURPOSTER'

THE HOUSE OF BERNARDA ALBA

THE PLAY — 'THE MAIDS'